THE TREASURES OF WITCH HAT MOUNTAIN

Other Avon Camelot Books by
Lou Kassem

A HAUNTING IN WILLIAMSBURG
MIDDLE SCHOOL BLUES
SECRET WISHES

LOU KASSEM is the author of seven books for young people including the award-winning *Listen for Rachel* which is available from Avon Flare. She is the mother of four grown daughters and currently lives in Blacksburg, Virginia, with her husband.

THE TREASURES OF WITCH HAT MOUNTAIN

LOU KASSEM

AN AVON CAMELOT BOOK

THE TREASURES OF WITCH HAT MOUNTAIN is an original publication of
Avon Books. This work has never before appeared in book form.

AVON BOOKS
A division of
The Hearst Corporation
1350 Avenue of the Americas
New York, New York 10019

First Avon Camelot Printing: October 1992
First Avon Camelot Special Printing: September 1992

CAMELOT TRADEMARK REG. U.S. PAT. OFF. AND IN OTHER COUNTRIES, MARCA
REGISTRADA, HECHO EN U.S.A.

Printed in the U.S.A.

OPM   10   9   8   7   6   5   4   3   2   1

This book is dedicated to everyone who ever wanted to find a secret treasure

Contents

Chapter One

Road to Adventure

"There it is! It looks just like a witch's hat, doesn't it? See how that pointy peak sticks up between those flat hills? Hey, there it is again! See?"

"Please, Cassie. You're rupturing my eardrums," Mrs. Black said, holding an ear.

"Sorry, Mom."

One of the twins grabbed Cassie's T-shirt and hauled her into the backseat.

"Jeez, Dad, don't drive so slow," Cassie begged.

"Don't you dare go any faster on these winding roads, Marcus."

"I'm being careful, Ann." The car crept forward at a snail's pace.

"Just cool it, motormouth," Jason said to Cassie. "We'll be there soon, so stop bugging Dad."

"I sure hope so," Justin grumbled. "I feel like a pretzel."

With a sigh, Cassie squinched in between her older brothers. The trouble with her practical, talented family was that they had absolutely no sense of adventure! Whereas she, the odd one out, could hardly wait. Something special was bound to happen at a place called Witch Hat Mountain. Trying to curb her impatience, she sat back and thought about the night that started them on the road to adventure. . . .

"Answer the door bell, please, Cassie. And, if it's one of the students, remind them that this is our dinner hour."

"Sure, Mom."

A hooded, cloaked figure stood in the shadows of the porch light. "Is this Professor Black's residence?"

"Yes, it is."

"Good. May I come in?"

Thinking it was a trick by one of the Greyfriars boys, Cassie smiled and stood aside. The dark figure swept past her. The hood fell back, revealing a sharp-faced old woman with piercing green eyes. Cassie's heart did a peculiar flip-flop. This was no trick.

"Good evening," the old woman said. "I'm your great-aunt Twyla Black. You must be Cassandra."

Cassie nodded, openmouthed. She'd never heard of an aunt Twyla—great or otherwise. On closer inspection, she knew this woman was definitely a relative. The black hair that came to a widow's peak on her forehead proclaimed her kinship. All the Blacks—Grampa, Dad, the twins, and Cassie—had this distinctive mark.

A smile softened the ancient, angular face. "Are you well named, Cassandra?"

"Pardon me?"

"Your name comes from Greek mythology. Cassandra was the prophetess who saw the truth, but no one listened to her."

Cassie returned the smile. "Even a Greek goddess would have a hard time getting this family to listen."

"Who is it, Cassie?" Mrs. Black called.

"Great-aunt Twyla Black," Cassie answered, looking up at their visitor and seeing her own sense of mischief reflected in those green eyes. "Come meet the family, Aunt Twyla."

Cassie's unflappable father was definitely flapped. He barely remembered his father mentioning an older sister.

"That's quite natural, Marcus," Aunt Twyla said reassuringly. "Charles ran away and joined the army when he was very young. He lost touch with the family. However, I kept track of him and of you."

"Then you know Dad died two years ago?"

"Yes, I knew, but unfortunately not until after his funeral. I'm afraid I waited too long to renew family ties. That's why, when I happened to be in Baltimore on business, I decided to call on you. I hope it isn't too inconvenient."

"Of course it isn't," Mrs. Black said, and invited Aunt Twyla to stay for dinner.

"I'd be delighted. My plane doesn't leave until nine-forty. This will give us time to get acquainted."

During dinner Cassie gave Aunt Twyla a see-what-I-mean look as her family, with very little prompting, talked of their busy lives. Her father spoke of Greyfriars Academy and even of the book he hoped to write one day. Her mother admitted the paintings on the wall were hers, explaining that she taught art history at the local community college and painted in her spare time. The twins rattled on and on about high school and their plans to attend Princeton in the fall . . . on full scholarships.

Cassie knew her turn was coming and dreaded it. She had nothing to add to the list of accomplishments. She didn't write books or paint pictures. And there was very little chance she'd ever earn a scholarship. She wasn't into academic stuff. So far, she'd found school B-O-R-I-N-G. Before Aunt Twyla could ask her questions, Cassie jumped in with some of her own. "Where do you live and what do you do, Aunt Twyla?"

"I have a home in the mountains of Virginia, Cassandra. I'm a naturalist. I study animals and plants in their natural habitats."

"What kind of animals?"

Every one of Aunt Twyla's answers provoked another question. Cassie could have listened to her all night.

"You're fortunate to have such a peaceful place to live and work," Mr. Black said, returning to the room after the fourth phone interruption. "I can't imagine why my father ever left."

"It's a long story," Aunt Twyla replied.

"Marcus is envious of the tranquillity you spoke of," Mrs. Black explained. "Living on campus, we rarely have a moment to ourselves."

4

"We're supposed to have summers off," Mr. Black grumbled, "but something always turns up."

"Living off the beaten path isn't for everyone," Aunt Twyla said as a car honked out front. "My goodness, there's my taxi. I'm glad I swallowed my manners and came to call."

"So are we," Mrs. Black said.

"Stop by Greyfriars any time you're in Baltimore, Aunt Twyla."

"Can't you stay a little longer?" asked Cassie.

"No, Cassandra. I have to get back to my mountain," Aunt Twyla replied. And, donning the ancient cloak, she disappeared into the dark.

"You have some strange relatives, Dad," Jason said.

"Yeah, she was even stranger than Grampa," Justin agreed.

Cassie, who hadn't cared much for their stiff, stern grandfather, protested. "I don't think she was strange, just interesting and different. I hope she visits again."

"I liked her, too, Cassie," Mrs. Black said. "But don't count on another visit. She has to be well into her eighties. Traveling must be difficult for her."

"Your mother's right, Cassie. The visit was welcome, but I doubt if we'll ever hear from Aunt Twyla again."

"Yes, we will," Cassie said stubbornly.

But February and March slipped past without a word. And the Blacks' predictable, busy, basically ordinary lives went on.

Then on April 1 Cassie's father came home looking as if he'd been hit by a Mack truck. "Family council," he called loudly.

Obeying the family's standing rule, everyone stopped whatever he or she was doing and came on the double. Anyone could call a council to discuss serious matters. Cassie had never had an occasion to do so, although she'd been the subject of one or two.

"Greyfriars is closing at the end of the term," Mr. Black announced.

After a moment of stunned silence, Jason laughed. "Okay, Dad, you got us. April fool! Right?"

"I'm afraid not, Jason. I've just come from a meeting of the board of trustees. Greyfriars is declaring bankruptcy. All faculty houses are to be vacated by June first."

"But that only gives us two months, Marcus."

"I know. This place will be a zoo," Mr. Black predicted.

He was right. From that day on, everything was in an uproar. The Black house was always full of strident students and frazzled faculty. Everyone was trying to find a home.

One Saturday morning in May a registered letter came for her father. He read it through twice, looking puzzled.

"What is it, Marcus? Another job offer?"

"No. It's a letter from some attorneys in Abingdon,

6

Virginia. Frawley, Frawley & Frawley. Aunt Twyla has died and left us her home.''

"How much is it worth?" asked the twins in unison.

"I don't know. There's a catch. We have to live at Blackhaven for three months before we can claim the inheritance.''

"Blackhaven?"

"I gather that's the name of the Black homestead. It's on Witch Hat Mountain, near a town called Trinity.''

"What happens if we don't go, Marcus?''

"It all goes to the National Wildlife Foundation," he answered, reading from the letter.

"Hey, you don't turn down a gift, Mom," Justin said.

"Not without looking at it," added Jason.

Cassie remembered Aunt Twyla's talk. "Can we go? Blackhaven sounds neat, Dad.''

"A vacation in the mountains wouldn't be bad, Marcus.''

"Only practical thing to do is scope it out, Dad.''

Her father made a wry face. "The only decent job offer I've had is the Vermont one. It doesn't begin until late September. We need somewhere to live this summer. I guess a mountain cabin is as good as any place.''

A thrill of anticipation shot through Cassie. Something told her this was going to be an unbelievable summer. . . .

*   *   *

7

Cassie leaned forward again. Here they were, winding through the mountains, she thought. Careful to keep her voice low, she asked, "Are we almost there?"

"Turn right at the Trinity signpost," Mrs. Black said, looking at the map. "I wish William Frawley weren't in the hospital. I'd feel better with a guide."

"At least his office had the electricity turned on and provided a map," Mr. Black said. "Ah! There's the mailbox." He swung the car into an overgrown lane.

The pointed mountain loomed above them, looking slightly forbidding. Everyone was silent as the car bumped down the rutted road. Suddenly the road flared into a wide circle. In the center of a huge clearing stood their home for the summer. Everyone got out of the car and stared.

Blackhaven was white. A peeling, dingy white. Five stone chimneys poked through its green tin roof. A wide porch was wrapped around the front and side of the two-story frame house. The side without a porch had a round, towerlike structure filled with windows. Everywhere grass, flowers, and weeds grew in tangled profusion.

"It's huge."

"Yeah, I expected a log cabin."

"It's pretty run-down," Mrs. Black said disappointedly.

"Let's go see what the inside looks like," Mr. Black said.

How could they be so calm? Who cared if it was old and shabby? This place was neat! Cassie bounded up the stone steps. "Come on, slowpokes. This is an adventure."

Chapter Two

At Last, a Letter

Mr. Black inserted a long, thin key into the lock and flung open the door. A wave of warm, stale air greeted them as they crowded into the wide hall.

"Marcus, look at this cupboard! It must be over a hundred years old."

Her father was concerned with more practical matters. "The electricity's on," he said, flipping a switch. "Let's see what the rest of the place is like."

"This is great!" Cassie cried, whirling through the downstairs rooms while her brothers opened drapes and windows.

"Actually, except for being dusty and old-fashioned, everything looks to be in very good order," Mrs. Black remarked.

"It's certainly livable," Mr. Black said. "Let's unload the car."

"Bring in the groceries first, please, Marcus."

"Wait!" Cassie cried. "There's a letter on the dining room table. It's addressed to you, Dad."

Her father took the letter, inspecting it carefully.

"It's from Aunt Twyla, isn't it? Read it out loud, Dad."

Mr. Black opened the envelope, cleared his throat, and began:

"My dear nephew,

"If you are reading this, you have already decided to honor an old woman's whim. Perhaps I should say selfish desire. No matter. You are here at Blackhaven, where three generations of Blacks have lived. You and your family are the last of our line. And that is the reason for my strange bequest.

"As you know, your father (my brother, Charles) was ashamed of his background. And, as soon as he could manage it, he left these mountains and his heritage. He did so in anger, and pride would not let him return. That was his choice and he had every right to make it.

"However, as a student of nature, I feel that a person's roots are as important as a plant's. That is why I asked you to come and live at Blackhaven for three months. After your stay, you may do whatever you wish with your inheritance.

"As Mr. William has probably told you, my business in Baltimore was with Johns Hopkins Medical Center. Their opinion agreed with my own

11

doctor's. Thus, I was given only a few months to put my affairs in order and check into the local hospital. I hope you will come to understand my reasons for this bequest. There are treasures here. I hope you find them. Perhaps Mr. Micawber will help you. I know Mr. William Frawley will assist you in any way possible—under the terms of my will.

> *"With affection,*
> *"Aunt Twyla Black*
> *"Postscriptum: My best regards to Ann, Jason, Justin, and Cassandra."*

Mr. Black put down the letter, shaking his head. "Well!"

A zillion questions flew through Cassie's head. She picked one. "Who's Mr. Micawber?"

"The only Micawber I know is a character in Dickens's *David Copperfield*," her father replied. "My guess is this one's probably a local handyman."

"Aunt Twyla said Mr. Micawber would help us find the treasures."

Mrs. Black shook her head and smiled. "I don't believe she meant real treasure, Cassie. She meant intangible things, like the beauty of nature."

"Is that what you think, Dad?"

"I don't know, kitten. Right now, I'm too tired to think. Let's get things unpacked and have some dinner."

"Well, I think Aunt Twyla meant exactly what she said! There are real treasures here. All we have to do is find them," Cassie declared stubbornly.

Jason and Justin rolled their eyes and grinned. "Here she goes again," Justin said. "Get ready for another of Cassie's flights of fantasy."

"While you're digging up the yard don't forget to dig out all those weeds," Jason said.

"Stop teasing, boys," ordered Mrs. Black. "We have work to do. Grab some of those groceries, Cassie. I'll fix some soup and sandwiches for dinner."

Cassie glared at her brothers and stomped out. After she took two bags to her mother she grabbed her suitcase and ran upstairs to pick out a bedroom. She inspected all four. "I have dibs on the end bedroom . . . the one with all the windows," she shouted.

"Sez who?" Jason asked, coming upstairs with a load of boxes.

"Sez me. First come, first served. Aunt Twyla's room is on the other end. Her stuff's still in there."

Jason peered in Aunt Twyla's room but chose another one. Mr. Black did the same thing.

I guess no one wants to bother Aunt Twyla, Cassie thought. Even if no one else in her family would never admit to such flights of fantasy, Cassie felt as if the room had a do not disturb sign on the door.

At the dinner table, Jason said, "Dad, Justin and I have been thinking. What if we fixed up this place? Like painted it. You know?"

"We'd sure get a better price for it when we sell," Justin added.

"Supplies wouldn't cost much, Dad."

"Well, I don't know . . ."

"It would give us something to do."

"I could fix up some of the inside," volunteered Mrs. Black. "I'd like to catalog these antiques anyway. With proper accreditation they'll be worth something, Marcus."

After a moment's consideration, Mr. Black said, "All right, we'll do it . . . with one stipulation: I get to work on my book half of every day."

"We'll all work only a half day," Mrs. Black said. "This is vacation time."

"Done!" said the twins.

"What can I do?" Cassie asked, feeling left out.

"Hunt for the treasure, of course," Jason said, laughing.

"You can help me, Cassie," her mother said, frowning at Jason.

"Let's take a look around and see what needs to be done," proposed Jason.

Cassie chose to tag along with her father and brothers.

Blackhaven held another surprise. The small room off the kitchen wasn't a pantry but a fully equipped mini-laboratory. While her brothers marveled at all the neat stuff, Cassie glanced out the window. "Oh! Look at that," she said, pointing to the tiny stone house built into the side of the mountain. "It's a troll house!"

Her brothers thought this was very funny. "Aren't you a little old to believe in fairy tale monsters, Cass?" teased Justin.

"I believe that's a springhouse, Cassie," explained her father. "People used them to keep food cold before refrigeration. Now, let's get down to business, boys."

Blushing, Cassie went to help her mother.

Sleep didn't come easily that night. Cassie tossed and turned while the old house creaked and groaned. The night was so black she could barely see her windows. It was rather spooky, but that wasn't what kept her awake. It seemed she never could say the right thing! Sometimes she felt like a useless fifth wheel in the family. Thoughts flew through her brain. Her brothers always teased her about her vivid imagination. Someday she'd show them she wasn't the oddball, that she wasn't silly. Maybe she'd discover Aunt Twyla's treasures. Wouldn't that be awesome? What could they be? Cassie wondered. And where? Who was Mr. Micawber? What if Mr. William Frawley had some vital clues and died before he could tell them? Things certainly hadn't gone exactly as Aunt Twyla planned! Mr. William was sick. Mr. Micawber was missing. And her family didn't believe there were any real treasures. Well, she did. And tomorrow—if it ever came—she would begin her search.

Chapter Three

Watcher in the Woods

"Let's inventory the house while the men are out from under foot, Cassie," Mrs. Black said, grabbing a pad and paper.

"Let's start upstairs."

"Fine by me."

When they came to Aunt Twyla's room, Mrs. Black raised her hand as if to knock.

Cassie giggled.

Her mother blushed. "That was silly, wasn't it?"

"Not really. I felt the same way last night when I peeked in. It feels like Aunt Twyla's still here."

"Then we're both silly, aren't we?" Mrs. Black said, laughing.

Aunt Twyla's room was large and comfortable. A four-poster bed with matching wardrobe and nightstand occupied one end of the room. A rolltop desk and chair sat in front of one of the large windows. An easy chair and reading lamp were drawn up in front of the huge stone fireplace. Floor-to-ceiling, packed bookcases flanked each side of the fireplace.

While her mother oohed and aahed over the furniture, Cassie thumped the walls for secret passages and checked for loose stones around the fireplace. Nothing!

It was the same for each of the other eight rooms. Mrs. Black found treasures. Cassie found none.

Finally, Mrs. Black said, "Honey, your treasure hunting is driving me crazy. Since the men aren't back yet, I think I'll set up my easel in the library/sun room; Daddy can use the little back room for his office."

"Good. I'm going to scope out the grounds."

"Don't go far from the house, Cassie. You might get lost."

"Oh, Mom!"

"I'm serious. There aren't any street signs out here. One tree looks pretty much like another."

"I'll be careful. I promise."

It didn't take long to check out the other buildings. The garage was full of tools, an old tractor, and assorted junk that hadn't been moved in years. To the side of the garage was an unpainted shack, empty except for large metal hooks hanging over a blackened fire pit. Probably a smokehouse, Cassie thought. The miniature stone house was a springhouse. It held nothing but cobwebs and the water flowing through a trough in the floor. The woodshed yielded no secrets either. What next?

17

Several small paths led off into the woods like spokes on a wheel. Should she try one? No, remembering her promise, she started down the lane toward the mailbox. Halfway down she spotted another overgrown road. Surely she couldn't get lost on this wide, tree-shaded lane. Besides, a road had to lead somewhere, didn't it?

She ambled along until the road ended abruptly at a moss-covered rock wall. Behind the wall, she saw ragged rows of rough stones and smooth slabs of marble peeking up from hordes of daisies and black-eyed Susans. A cemetery!

Cassie tiptoed inside. One grave looked newer than the rest. She went over to read the marble marker. TWYLA DAWN BLACK was all that was on it. She strolled through the peaceful grounds trying to read some of the other stones. It was so quiet she could hear the bees hum in the flowers. Her mom would like to paint this scene.

Suddenly the hairs on the back of her neck stood up. A creepy feeling swept up Cassie's spine. She *knew* she was being watched. Cassie spun around, calling, "Who's there?"

Silence.

Nothing moved. But the feeling grew. "Who's there?" she cried again. Cassie heard a branch snap. To her it was as loud as a gun. She turned and ran for home. Cassie didn't stop until she entered the clearing and saw the twins unloading the car.

"You're just in time to lend a hand," Jason said.

Justin was more observant. "What's the matter, Cass? Was a troll chasing you?" he teased.

Cassie had been going to tell them about the watcher in the woods, but quickly changed her mind. No use giving those two more ammunition. "Did you get everything we need?"

"No," her father answered, "but the man at the hardware store said they'd get the rest in Abingdon and deliver it tomorrow."

"That's the longest speech anyone made," Justin said. "Everyone stared at us like we were from outer space."

"Maybe they aren't used to strangers," Mrs. Black called from the porch. "Lunch is ready when you are."

"Did you ask about Mr. Micawber?" Cassie asked her father as they went inside.

"No, I didn't, kitten. Maybe next time . . . when the natives aren't so restless."

"I'm sure they were just curious, Marcus."

They aren't the only ones, Cassie thought. But she kept quiet.

The next morning they'd just finished breakfast when a truck rumbled up the drive. "Mornin'," said a man, hopping down from the cab. "Name's Bandy. I got your order."

Mr. Bandy was a stocky man with a face resembling

an English walnut. A red baseball cap rode firmly on his ears. Cassie thought he looked a little like a modern-day troll, but didn't say so.

When she offered to help unload the truck, Mr. Bandy gave her a snaggle-toothed smile. "No, missy. This here's a man's job."

Cassie grinned at her brothers and sat on the steps to watch. Finally, the twins carried the last load to the garage and Mr. Black went inside for his checkbook. Mr. Bandy wiped his face with a large red bandana. "Sure is hot."

"Would you like a cold drink?" Cassie asked.

"That'd hit the spot, by cracky."

"Have a seat. I'll be right back."

"Don't mind if I do."

When Cassie returned with a cold drink, Mr. Bandy downed it in two long gulps. "Much obliged, missy. You folks gonna do all the work yourselves, huh?"

"I guess so. Unless we can find Mr. Micawber. Do you know him?"

"Micawber? No, I don't recollect anybody by that name in these parts."

"Is there *anybody* in these parts? I didn't see any houses when we came in."

"Nobody up this way 'cept the Coles over in Cole Holler. I wouldn't have no truck with them, was I you."

Mrs. Black, coming out with a check in her hand, heard his remark, "What's the matter with the Coles?"

Mr. Bandy chuckled. "They're not too sociable." Then seeing Mrs. Black's frown, he added, "Don't worry, ma'am. They won't cross that there split-rail fence markin' your property. Coles keep to theyselves. You all best do the same." He took the check, tipped his fingers to his hat, and drove off.

"Did you hear that, Cassie? You are to stay on our side of the fence. And the Coles—whoever they are—will stay on theirs."

"Yes, Mother," Cassie answered. Meaning that she'd heard. Not that she wouldn't stray. After all, she was pretty sure the Coles had already broken their half of the bargain. Maybe these antisocial Coles knew Mr. Micawber.

Chapter Four

Not Catching a Cole

"Enough already with the treasure hunt! I can't hear myself think."

"Sorry, Dad."

Cassie grabbed a book and ran outside. She'd been knocking on the walls to check for secret passages. Whatever Aunt Twyla had hidden she'd hidden well. Not even the mini-laboratory off the kitchen held any secrets.

Sighing, she escaped down one of the now-familiar paths into the woods. In the past few weeks she had explored each of these strange trails. They led to the split-rail fence and stopped. The trails didn't seem to have a purpose. So far, she hadn't had the nerve to climb the rocky, tangled peak of Witch Hat. It looked dangerous. Besides, she could swear she'd seen something moving around in the trees up there. And sometimes she still felt those eyes watching her.

Plopping down under a huge oak, she tried to figure out what to do next. "I'm stuck, Aunt Twyla. I can't find your treasure. Heck, I can't even find Mr. Micawber. I need help . . . a clue . . . something."

A large blackbird flew down and perched on a branch across from her. "Caw, caw, caw," it scolded.

"Shoo!" Cassie yelled, waving her arms.

The bird looked at her, then flew away. Like most of the animals at Blackhaven it didn't seem afraid of people. Even the squirrels in the backyard would come up to your feet for food.

She had picked up her book and started to read when a long, low whistle came from behind her. A soft voice called, "Here-y-cup. Here-y-cup."

Cassie peeked around the tree. Someone was moving carefully through the tangle of laurel. "Hey, you! Come out of there," she cried, jumping to her feet.

A girl with long blond hair popped up like a Jill-in-the-box. Her big blue eyes were wide with fright. "O-o-o-h," she moaned. Then she ran.

Cassie ran after her. "Wait . . . wait a minute."

The girl ran like a deer. She leaped the split-rail fence in a single bound.

Cassie followed, yelling, "Wait!" or "Stop!" every few breaths.

The girl ran faster, sometimes disappearing altogether.

Cassie kept up the chase. She was sure she'd found her watcher.

Suddenly the path was blocked by a figure waving a

big stick. Cassie skidded to a halt. Not because of the stick. The girl had changed into a boy!

"Go back on your own land," he ordered.

"How'd you do that?" Cassie gasped, holding her aching sides.

His blue eyes narrowed. "Do what?"

"Change into a boy."

A giggle came from somewhere in the bushes.

"Didn't," he replied.

"Ask her about Hiccup," said a small voice.

"No."

A girl—an exact copy of the boy, except for the length of hair—emerged from behind a tree. She gave her twin a scornful look. "Could you use your powers to find Hiccup?" she asked timidly.

"Who are you? What's a hiccup? What powers?"

The boy and girl backed away from her rapid questions.

"I'm Davey Cole," the boy said defiantly.

"I'm Daisy. Cousin Lutie's dog got lost. We have to find him. He's black and white. Name's Hiccup. Have you seen him?"

Cassie shook her head. "I haven't seen a dog. How long has he been missing?"

"Two days," the twins answered.

"Two days? Hah! You've been spying on me a lot longer than that!"

"No, we haven't!" they said in unison.

"Well, somebody's been following me around in the woods."

24

"Maybe it's Miss Twyla's ghost."

"Hush, Daisy!"

"Now wait just a darned minute," Cassie said, shaking her fist at them. The minute her hand went up the twins turned and ran.

"Hey, wait . . ." Her words hung on empty air. For a moment she wondered if she had imagined the twins. Only the crackling of the underbrush in the distance reassured her that she'd been talking to real people.

A more immediate problem surfaced. She had no idea where she was. Which way was Blackhaven? She turned in circles. Nothing looked familiar. She'd run a long way into the woods. Which way was home? Cassie began to panic. She had a terrible urge to run again. To anywhere. She just wanted out of the woods which no longer seemed friendly. Blood pounded in her ears. She felt dizzy . . . and that noisy crow was cawing at her. . . . She fixed her eyes on the bird and grabbed hold of a tree. The ground stopped spinning. "I—I hope you know the way home."

As an answer, the crow flew a few feet away and perched on another limb.

Cassie followed and eventually came to a section of the fence. She crossed over and found a path that led home.

The crow disappeared.

She was bursting to tell someone about the twins but couldn't. They were *Coles*. She'd been told not to associate with them. What's more, she'd disobeyed and gone off Black property.

Something else was bugging her. Her feathered friend. She didn't know much about birds, but she was sure the crow's behavior was unusual.

That evening when her parents were relaxing in the living room, Cassie said casually, "Dad, what do you know about birds?"

"Not much. What kind of bird?"

"A crow, I think."

"I believe there are some books on birds in my studio," her mother said.

"Good. I'll check it out."

"Be careful of my canvas. It isn't dry."

"I will."

She went to the library/studio and found a book with a picture that certainly looked like her bird—all glossy and black. The book said crows were highly intelligent, gregarious, and adaptable. They ate both animal and vegetable matter. And were well known for their thievish habits. It didn't say anything about their attaching themselves to people or being guide birds. It also didn't say they couldn't.

As she replaced the bird book, she noticed two books with T. D. Black on their spines. Just as she pulled them out, a clap of thunder shook the whole house. Cassie grabbed the books and ran.

"Did you find your book?" her father asked.

"Uh-huh. Dad, tell me about Mr. Micawber. The guy in *David Copperfield*, I mean. What was he like?"

"Mr. Micawber was one of Dickens's best drawn

characters. He was something of a con artist, popping up at the most unexpected times in David Copperfield's life. Why the sudden interest in Dickens, kitten?''

With an effort, Cassie suppressed a grin. "Just curious. Look what else I found. Two books written by Aunt Twyla.''

"Really? Let's see.''

Together, they pored over *A Naturalist in the Blue Ridge* and *Appalachian Flora and Fauna*.

"See, Cassie, I told you this place was a treasure in itself,'' Mrs. Black said.

"The paths that lead into the woods are probably observation trails,'' her father said. "I'm quite impressed. Aunt Twyla was a serious scholar.''

"Sure, she was,'' Cassie said, looking at a picture of a mushroom called Destroying Angel. Inside she was laughing. Aunt Twyla may have been a serious scholar, but she also had a sense of humor. Cassie was certain her clever flying friend was named Mr. Micawber after the Dickens character.

A streak of lightning lit up the sky, causing the lights to flicker. "We'd better check the windows,'' Mrs. Black said. "I think we're in for a major storm.''

The storm broke and was still raging when they went up to bed. Cassie covered her head with a pillow and prayed it would end by morning. She had so many things to do: check out the crow, find the twins, ask about her supposed powers . . .

Chapter Five

Hiccup

By morning the rain had stopped and the sun shone brightly in a cloudless blue sky.

"It's too wet to paint the house," Mr. Black said. "We'll have to reverse our schedule today . . . if we get to paint at all."

"I could use a break," Mrs. Black said. "I think I'll run into Trinity and see if I can get a haircut. Want to come with me, Cassie? Your hair has gotten very long. I know it must be hot."

"No, thanks. It isn't hot if I keep it in a ponytail. I'm going exploring again."

"Wear a jacket. The woods are wet."

Mothers! Cassie rolled her eyes and nodded. She grabbed her green windbreaker from the hall rack.

Mrs. Black went out, jingling the car keys in her hand. "Be careful. Stay on our property."

Cassie smiled and waved, but didn't promise anything.

As soon as her mom drove off, she ran outside and scanned the trees. The noisy crow was nowhere in sight.

"Looking for flying saucers?" Jason asked on his way to the garage.

"No, just checking the weather. What are you two going to do today?"

"Tinker with the tractor we found in the garage," Justin said.

"What for?"

"So we can mow these weeds."

"Jeez. I thought you guys only knew about modern stuff like computers."

"Oh, get lost, brat!"

"Thanks, I think I will," Cassie said, grinning. She picked a trail and marched off into the woods. When she was a good distance from the house, she left the trail and plunged deeper among the trees. Stepping into a laurel thicket, she cried, "Oh-oh-oh, I'm lost. How do I get back home?" She felt pretty silly, but she was sure her plan would work. She called again and waited to be rescued.

No crow came.

She went further and called again. Only her echo answered. After a few more tries, she gave up and sat down on a stump to eat the biscuit she'd brought for the crow. The woods were silent except for an occasional *splat-splat* of water from the leaves. She was glad she'd worn her windbreaker. "Where is that dumb bird when I want him?"

29

A strange sound answered her. Not the grating call of the crow, but a faint whimper. Cassie held her breath, listening. There it was again. She puckered her lips and whistled. Then she called, "Here, Hiccup."

Faint yelps answered her. She followed them down a steep hillside and into a gully. Near a big pile of rocks lay a little black-and-white dog. His tail thumped a feeble welcome.

"Poor Hiccup, you're hurt, aren't you?" she murmured, bending down to pat his head.

Hiccup gave her hand a wet lick. Now she wished she hadn't eaten that biscuit. Hiccup was bound to be hungry after three days. What should she do? Go for Dad or try to find Daisy and Davey? She decided on the twins. She was closer to their land. Taking off her jacket, Cassie put it around the little dog. "This will keep you warm and dry till I get help."

Hiccup whined pitifully and tried to follow her as she walked away. She couldn't leave him. She went back and crouched beside him. Hiccup looked at her with trust-filled eyes. Every time her hand came close to his muzzle, he licked it.

Okay. What now? On the hill above her was the split-rail fence. She knew she had to cross over it to find the twins. "All right, Hiccup. I don't know exactly how to get there, but I'm taking you home." With the little dog wrapped in her windbreaker, she started off in the general direction of where she'd last seen the twins.

After a few minutes, she heard a strange roaring. It

grew louder and louder the further she walked. When she came around a sharp turn she saw what was making the noise. A river roared through a rocky gap between two mountains. Across the gap stretched a rope-and-plank bridge. In the distance, on the other side, a spiral of white smoke rose into the blue sky.

Hiccup wriggled in her arms.

"That's home, huh?"

He tried to lick her chin.

"Okay. I get the message. Daisy! Davey!" She yelled until she was hoarse, but the raging water drowned out her cries.

The bridge did not look safe. The ropes were frayed and some of the planks had buckled. What was below the bridge looked worse. It wasn't far to the other side though. And she could see a path leading toward the smoke. This had to be the way Daisy and Davey had come yesterday.

She stepped onto the bridge.

Nothing happened.

She took a few more shuffling steps.

Still nothing.

Hiccup seemed to have gained weight. Her arms felt as if they were going to drop off. She had to get across before they gave way. She took four quick, normal steps.

The bridge began to sway.

The rocking motion made her sick to her stomach. She froze. She was afraid to go forward or backward.

31

A sour taste rose in her throat. Cassie let the bridge stop swinging. She didn't know whether to turn back or keep going. The river roared, and Cassie looked at the water raging below. "Help," she whispered to herself.

Hiccup whined and licked her chin.

Closing her eyes, Cassie took a deep breath and ran. When her feet touched solid ground she almost fainted with relief. Her relief was very short. As she opened her eyes, a bearded giant stepped out of the woods. He rushed toward her, sunlight glinting off his upraised axe.

The axe descended.

Cassie's knees buckled . . .

Chapter Six

The Bad Coles

The giant caught her before she hit the ground. "You okay?" he growled.

Cassie had never fainted before, so she wasn't sure. "I—I think so. How's Hiccup?"

The man let go of her and stooped to pick up his axe. "I caught the both of you." His eyes glittered as brightly as his axe. "Where'd you find him?"

Cassie licked her dry lips and waved vaguely toward the bridge. "Over there. I think some rocks fell on him. His back legs are hurt."

"Uh-huh," the man said, looking at her suspiciously. "Move along then. We'll see to you both."

She didn't have any choice. His bulky body blocked her retreat. Besides, she didn't care to cross that swinging bridge again.

Hiccup whimpered softly from the cradle of the giant's arm. "Lutie's gonna be mighty happy to see you, little fellow," the man said.

When he spoke to Hiccup his voice was gentle. That, at least, was comforting. But what did he mean by "he'd see to her?" He sounded angry. He had an axe. No one knew where she was. . . . "I'm Cassandra Black," she said, looking over her shoulder.

"Roscoe Cole. Watch where you're walking!"

Cassie stumbled, turned around, and hurried on. She could feel his eyes boring into her back.

Like corks out of a bottle, Cassie and Roscoe popped out of the woods. Below them was a higgledy-piggledy log structure. It was the strangest looking house— or group of houses—she'd ever seen.

There were people sitting on the porch of the center building. As soon as they were spotted, a girl dumped something from her lap and hobbled to meet them. "Uncle Roscoe! You found Hiccup. Is he hurt?"

In the same gentle voice he'd used with Hiccup, Mr. Cole said, "He's just bunged up his hind legs, Lutie. Don't get all het up."

As Lutie rushed past, Cassie noticed her right foot was horribly deformed.

"Let me see. Put him down, Uncle Roscoe."

"In a minute, Lutie. Mind your manners. This gal brought Hiccup home."

"Thank you, miss," Lutie said, blushing and trying to hide her bad foot behind her good leg.

"You're welcome. I'm glad I found him."

By now several other people had gathered around the

porch. Cassie was relieved to see Daisy and Davey appear. "Hi," she shouted, waving to them. "I found Hiccup."

"Hi," they replied, looking uncomfortable.

Cassie was disappointed. She thought they'd be happy. She didn't have time to think about their reaction because, as they neared the porch, an old lady with about a million wrinkles on her face threw her apron over her head. She began rocking and moaning loudly.

A pretty blond woman, an adult version of the twins, stepped forward. "Hush now, Mam," she said calmly. "Roscoe, what have you brought home?"

"Hiccup and Cassandra Black. Seems she found the dog over to her place." He paused, glaring at the twins. "She knew his name and where he belonged."

Daisy and Davey looked intently at their toes.

The old lady groaned louder. She mumbled something under the cover of her apron.

"Why, thank you, Cassandra," the blond woman said. "Lutie's been half crazy with worry over her dog. I'm Dulcie Cole, mother of those twins. You come on up on the porch and visit a spell."

"She came across the swinging bridge," Roscoe Cole said. "Shook her up a mite. Way that bridge was a-swinging, I thought this gal was gonna be pitched into the river. I'll see to the dog." He and Lutie disappeared around the corner of the house.

Dulcie guided Cassie to a chair. "You do look kinda

green around the edges. That old bridge is dangerous. Stella, why don't you run and get a cup of coffee off the stove. Put lots of sugar in it.''

Cassie was grateful for the chair. Her legs felt as if they were made of Silly Putty. The other people—two teenage boys, the twins, and a grandmotherly woman—continued to stare at her as if she were from another planet.

Dulcie noticed. ''What's the matter with you-all?''

The apron woman mumbled louder and rocked harder.

''Oh, lordy! Mam's been telling tales again, hasn't she?'' Dulcie said, laughing.

The twins and the two boys nodded sheepishly.

''They're true! They're true! God help us all,'' the old woman shouted clearly.

''She don't mean no harm,'' the grandmotherly woman said.

Cassie was totally confused. Maybe she *had* dropped onto another planet. Dulcie sat down beside her. ''I know Mam doesn't mean any harm. But Cassandra here must think we're all crazy, backwoods dolts. She does us a favor and we treat her like poison ivy. Here,'' she said, handing Cassie the cup of coffee just given to her, ''drink this.''

Cassie took a sip of the dark, sweet brew. ''Please, just call me Cassie.''

''All right, Cassie. Now tell us how you came to find Hiccup. How'd you ever get him over here?''

Cassie sipped her coffee and told them. By the time she finished her tale and the coffee, she felt much better.

"I think you were very brave," Daisy said. "I wouldn't have crossed that ole bridge with a wriggly dog in my arms."

"You weren't supposed to cross the bridge *at all*," Dulcie said sharply. "Your daddy's told you that time and time again."

"But that's where Lutie said Hiccup went," Daisy protested.

"Lutie sure couldn't go after him," Davey added. "And if we hadn't gone over, then Cassie wouldn't have known where to bring him."

"All right!" Dulcie said, shaking her head and laughing. "Trying to catch you two out is like trying to catch the wind. Anyway, we're much obliged to you, Cassie."

"I'm glad I found him. I hope he'll be okay." A loud groan from the apron lady spurred her to her feet. "I'd better be going back now."

"Don't mind Mam," Dulcie said. "And you are *not* going like you came. Roscoe'll take you home in the truck as soon as he tends Hiccup."

"I'll take her back, Aunt Dulcie," volunteered one of the boys.

Dulcie laughed. "No, thanks, Riley. Going back with you could be more dangerous than crossing the bridge."

Everyone, except Riley, laughed.

"Riley got his driver's license last March," Daisy explained, "and he's already wrecked the truck twice. He drives too fast."

"Do not," Riley muttered, glaring at Daisy.

"Daisy, you and Davey show Cassie around the place. The rest of you get back to whatever you were doing," Dulcie said.

Daisy grabbed her hand. "Come on. We'll show you our house."

Cassie was happy to get away from the moaning old woman. The twins showed her through their neat log home. Neither of them volunteered an explanation of Mam's strange behavior, so she didn't ask questions. She admired their house and told them so.

"Dad built this himself," Davey said, "when we came up here to live."

"Then you haven't always lived here?"

"No. Only four years. When Uncle Bass—uh—went away," Daisy explained, "we had to come take care of the family. Before that we lived in Abingdon."

"Which place do you like best?"

"Here," Davey answered.

"Most of the time," Daisy said.

Davey nodded. "There's lots to do here. Except sometimes it's lots of the same thing."

"Are you going to live here full-time?" asked Daisy.

"Just for the summer. My dad's a professor. Wherever he takes a job is where we'll go."

The twins nodded understandingly.

"Let's show Cassie the swimming hole," Davey said.

"No, let's show her the basket factory."

Before they could decide, Roscoe Cole called, "Come along, girl. I'll take you home now."

"Can't she stay a little longer? We didn't show her half our stuff," Davey complained.

"Please, Daddy," begged Daisy.

"No. She goes back. Hop in the truck, miss."

As Cassie climbed into the battered blue pickup, Davey whispered, "Later," and motioned with his head toward the other side of the mountain.

Cassie got the message and nodded.

The twins smiled innocently.

Before they could drive away, Lutie hobbled over to the truck. "I'm beholden to you for savin' Hiccup," she said, smiling.

"Is he going to be all right?"

"Right as rain!"

Mr. Cole gunned the motor and Lutie stepped back. The truck bumped off down the dirt driveway.

"You don't have to do this. I could have walked back," Cassie said.

"Sure, you could've. You and the twins are cut out of the same cloth. Got more courage than sense. Crossing that rickety old bridge was a fool thing to do."

She didn't know how to deal with his anger. She wasn't hurt. Hiccup was safe. So why was he mad? She sat back and let him fume as they drove down the narrow, graveled road.

When they came to her drive, she said meekly, "You can let me out here, Mr. Cole. No need for you to go all the way up to the house."

Mr. Cole stopped the truck. He gave her a hard look. "You disobeyed orders, too, huh?"

Cassie blushed and nodded.

"Kids!" he said, shaking his head. "I call us even now, Miss Black."

Even? Miss Black? "Thank you for the ride, Mr. Cole," Cassie said, puzzled.

Mr. Cole nodded and drove away, throwing up a spray of gravel.

Cassie jogged up the lane. Her stomach told her it was past lunch, but she paid no attention to its grumbles. Mr. Bandy was right. The Coles weren't exactly sociable . . . at least, most of them weren't. But she liked the twins. They were her kind of people. How was she going to get away this afternoon to meet them?

Just as she came into the yard, Jason came out the door. "It's about time you showed up. Dad sent me out to look for you. Where've you been?"

"Out. I forgot the time."

"Forgot your jacket, too, didn't you?"

Too late, she remembered. "Oh, I know where I left it. I'll get it after lunch. Mom's not back yet either, is she?"

"You're in luck. Here she comes now."

"Hi, Mom. How'd it go?" Cassie called brightly.

"I got a haircut and an earful," Mrs. Black replied. She did not look happy.

40

"You mean someone actually talked to you?" Jason teased.

"Not exactly. I eavesdropped when they gossiped about our neighbors . . . those awful Coles. Let's go in and I'll share the horror stories."

Chapter Seven

Mr. Micawber

"One of the Coles is in prison for killing a man in a fist fight," Mrs. Black reported. "It seems our neighbors are notorious for fighting with fists, knives, and guns."

And maybe axes? Cassie added silently, repressing a shudder.

"They sound like dangerous characters," Mr. Black said.

"That isn't all. Evidently government agents have been trying for years to catch the Coles making illegal whiskey."

"You mean our neighbors are moonshiners?" Justin said.

Jason grinned. "Whoa! Did you hear all that in the beauty parlor, Mom?"

"Beauty parlors are the gossip centers of any community," Mrs. Black replied, laughing. "It was odd, though, how everyone clammed up when they learned who I was.''

"Then you got the respectful, silent treatment. Right?'' Jason said.

"Exactly. How did you know?''

"It's the same with us when we go into town.''

"Yeah, it's a mystery Jason and I are determined to solve,'' Justin said.

Cassie stuffed the last bite of her sandwich in her mouth and washed it down with milk. "May I be excused?''

"Just a minute,'' her father said. "I have a proposition. I propose we skip our painting for today. What do you say?''

"Great idea! Jason and I almost have that tractor going.''

"I'll finish my sketches of the cemetery.''

"Fine by me,'' Cassie said, edging toward the door. She grabbed a bag of corn chips and slipped out. All the news about the Coles was bad, but she didn't care. She wanted to see Daisy and Davey again.

They were waiting for her beside the fence. "We'd just about given up on you,'' Davey said.

"I brought your jacket,'' Daisy said.

"Thanks. I wasn't looking forward to crossing that bridge again. Or upsetting Mam.''

"Aw, don't pay any attention to her,'' Davey said. "She's almost a hundred years old. All she does is sit and rock and tell good stories.''

"Why did she throw her apron over her head?"

"She was afraid you'd give her the evil eye," Daisy answered.

"Me? Why?"

"You're a Black."

"So?"

"Your hair," began Daisy.

"Comes to a point. Just like Miss Twyla's," Davey finished. "Mam says all the Blacks are marked like that. It's a witch's mark."

"That's the dumbest thing I ever heard," Cassie said, laughing. "So how come you're not afraid?"

"We decided you weren't a witch."

"Witches don't do good things, like bring lost dogs home."

Cassie noted they were still on their side of the fence. She held out the bag of corn chips. "Well, you were right. Come on over and tell me about this witch thing. Does everyone around here think we're witches?"

Silently the twins looked at each other and seemed to agree. They crossed over. "Don't know about everybody," Davey said. "But Daddy said it was better to be safe than sorry." He took a large handful of chips and munched away.

Daisy took a smaller helping. "Mama laughed at him and said that was backwoodsy thinking."

"Daddy got mad and said she didn't know the whole story. There's bad blood between our families. Then he stomped off."

"What did he mean by bad blood?"

Davey shrugged. "We don't know."

"But we know how to find out," Daisy said, her eyes sparkling. "Mam will tell us."

"Then will you tell me?"

"Sure."

"You got a right to know, the way I figure," Davey said. "Come on, let's do something. Look for a grapevine, Daisy."

"You ever swing on a grapevine?" asked Daisy as they trotted after Davey.

"No, but I've read about vine swings. I found some of my brothers' Tarzan books when we were moving. Tarzan lived in the jungle and used vine swings."

"Did you bring the books with you?" Davey asked eagerly.

"Can we borrow them?" Daisy asked when Cassie nodded.

"Sure."

The whole afternoon was fun. The three of them explored on both sides of the fence. Finally, Davey looked up at the sky and announced, "Time to go. Mama will have supper near 'bout ready."

"We'll walk you back to the fence," offered Daisy. "It's easy to get turned around in these woods if you aren't used to them."

"We got lost so many times the first year we came up here that Daddy threatened to tie bells on us—like cows," Davey said indignantly.

Cassie was reluctant to part with her friends. "Can you come back tomorrow?"

"We don't know what chores we'll have."

"See, everybody has to help at our place," explained Davey. "Me and Daisy do our share."

"I have to help in the mornings, too," Cassie said, although she was sure no one would ever miss her efforts. "We ought to have some way to signal each other if we're busy. We don't have a phone."

"We don't either," said Daisy.

"Hey, we could use Indian signs," Davey ventured after a thoughtful pause. "They used rocks. Just plain ole rocks, stacked up in certain ways."

"Like a secret code?"

"Yeah. Like three rocks stacked up could mean we can't come today. Two rocks could mean—uh—wait for us," suggested Davey.

"We could work out more signs later," Daisy said.

They scurried around and found six smooth stones. Daisy placed three on her side of the fence and three on Cassie's. "There! See, they're just three old stones. I bet nobody would ever notice them."

"I'll bring a pencil and paper tomorrow and we can work up a whole set of secret messages," Cassie said.

"Don't forget the books you promised to loan us," Daisy reminded her.

"I won't. Don't you forget to question Mam about this feud."

"Mam loves to talk. Don't worry about that," Davey said. "Let's go, Daisy. I'm hungry."

Cassie walked slowly back to Blackhaven. She'd solved the mystery of why people treated Blacks so strangely. But how was she going to tell her family? She had a feeling she'd be in big trouble if they knew what she'd been up to.

The crow flew past her and lit on a branch over the path. "Er-caw-r-caw-r," he scolded as he paced up and down on the limb.

Cassie stopped dead in her tracks. "Mi-caw-ber? Mi-caw-ber? Is that your name?" She raised her arm slowly. "Come here, Mr. Micawber. Come down and see me."

With two swift flaps of his shiny wings, the crow flew down and perched on her bare arm. His expression seemed to say, Well, it certainly took you long enough.

He looked so funny, she couldn't help laughing.

Mr. Micawber flew back to his branch, giving her a reproachful look.

"I'm sorry. Please, come back."

"Caw-er-caw-caw," he scolded and flew away.

Cassie ran the rest of the way home. This news she could share!

Her parents were sitting on the front porch when she ran up, yelling, "I found him! I found him!"

"Catch your breath, honey," Mrs. Black said. "Found who?"

"Mr. Micawber. See, I got lost the other day and he led me home. Today he flew—"

"He flew?" her father asked with one eyebrow shooting up.

"When were you lost?" Mrs. Black asked with alarm.

"Not lost. Turned around. No big deal, Mom. See, I said, 'I'm lost. Which way to Blackhaven?' and he led me back to the fence. Neat, huh?"

"Where is this man, Cassandra? Where did he come from?" her mother demanded.

Cassie grinned. "No problem, Mom. Mr. Micawber's a bird. Not a man. Don't you get it? Mi-*caw*-ber. That's what he says. He sat on my arm today. But I laughed and he flew away."

Her brothers had come out to see what the excitement was. "A bird sat on your arm?" Jason said. "What kind of bird?"

"A crow. A big, black crow. Wait'll you see him. He's neat, guys."

Mr. Black cleared his throat. "This crow—Mr. Micawber—guided Cassie out of the woods, boys." A smile played hide-and-seek around his lips.

"Oh, a guide bird," Jason said. "Yes, I believe they are quite common in these parts."

"Of course they only appear to girls who can talk to birds, like our sister," Justin said.

"Boys," Mrs. Black warned, suppressing a smile.

"Well, I'll have to see this crow to believe it," Jason said. "You know this sounds like Cassie's pigtail story to me."

"No, it isn't!"

"Come on, Cass. Don't you remember the fit you

threw when you pulled a piece of rope out of the hole you were digging to China? You insisted you'd pulled off a Chinaman's pigtail. You even said you'd seen his poor bald head. You wouldn't stop crying until we went out—with flashlights and spades—to give the pigtail back. The bald Chinaman turned out to be a smooth rock.''

"I was just a little kid then!"

"You weren't such a little kid last year when you thought Professor Abedi was a Middle East terrorist.''

"I didn't know he was a professor. He left a ticking briefcase in the post office!"

"A timer for his lectures, as I recall," Justin said. "You cleared the area by yelling *'Bomb!'*''

Cassie blushed. "This is different. Mr. Micawber is real.''

"Sure, he is," Jason scoffed. "We all believe there's a bird that acts like a Saint Bernard.''

"Maybe you could show us Mr. Micawber in the morning," Mrs. Black said kindly.

Cassie was crushed. Her family thought she was making up stories again. Just wait until they saw Mr. Micawber. Then we'd see who had red faces!

Full of confidence, Cassie ran outdoors the next morning. She whistled and called until her throat ached. Mr. Micawber didn't show one black feather.

"That's our sister," Jason said. "The girl who talks to birds.''

"Ah-caw-caw," Justin mocked, laughing so hard he nearly fell off the roof.

Finally, Mr. Black said, "That's enough, boys. Cassie, stop that racket and bring me another can of paint from the garage."

Unfortunately, Cassie chose a can that had been opened. In her rush to be useful, she tripped and spilled half the paint.

Her father was understandably annoyed. "Go inside and help your mother, Cass. I'll clean up this mess."

"I don't have anything for you to do, honey. Not unless you know something about antiques," Mrs. Black said.

"I don't seem to know much about anything. Can I take my lunch out to the woods?"

"I suppose," her mother answered. "Be careful."

"Okay." Sighing, she slapped a sandwich together, stuffed some extra apples, four books, three pencils, and a pad of paper into her backpack. She went down the path, keeping an eye out for Mr. Micawber. She sure didn't want him to show up now! Daisy and Davey would really believe she was a witch if he popped up and lit on her arm again.

Chapter Eight

Of Witches and Indians

"Hi, have an apple," Cassie invited as the twins bounded up the path.

"Did you bring the books?" Davey asked, looking at the red delicious with a hungry eye.

"Sure. Pencils and paper, too. We can work on our secret codes while we eat. Did you get Mam to talk?"

Daisy rolled her eyes. "Did we ever!"

"Mam rambles a lot though," Davey added. "Then she falls asleep. Gettin' a whole story outta her is like pulling hen's teeth."

"I didn't know hens had teeth."

"They don't. So pulling them's impossible," Davey said, chomping a bite of apple.

"You didn't find out anything?"

"Oh, we did, too!" Daisy said, giving her brother a stern look. "It's kinda mixed up though."

"Seems like our families were on speaking terms

once, way back. Then they had a falling out because of Indians," explained Davey.

"Indians?"

"Uh-huh. Your great-great granddaddy was friendly with the Cherokees. Gave Indians free run of his land but not his white neighbors."

"That's when the fence was put up. Folks who didn't abide by Lucian Black's rules . . . well, bad luck happened to them," added Daisy.

"What kind of bad luck?"

"Oh, their animals ran off or took sick. Their cows went dry and their chickens stopped laying."

"Mam said people had mysterious accidents, too. They had bad falls or got terrible sick after riling a Black. That's what happened to Mam's husband, Albert," Daisy said.

"What happened to him?"

"Well—" began Daisy.

"Let me tell. See, great-granddaddy Albert went deer hunting. He wounded a deer and was tracking it on your land when a big storm came up. Albert took shelter in a cave and after the storm blew itself out came on home. Next day Thomas Black came over calling Albert a trespasser and a thief! Well, of course, Albert knocked him flat and sent him packin'. Thomas Black shouted an awful curse at Albert before he left. A week later Albert came down with a terrible sickness that crippled him for life."

"That doesn't make sense. Albert could have gotten sick on his own," Cassie protested.

"Yeah, but folks had begun to notice how sickness and bad luck followed anyone who crossed a Black. There were other things, too," Daisy said.

"What, for instance?"

Daisy lowered her voice to a whisper. "Well, for one thing, Thomas Black stood up before the whole congregation at Freewill Baptist Church and said the Bible wasn't word-for-word true! Made folks so mad they threw your whole family out of church, Miss Twyla and her brothers included."

"Yeah, folks said Thomas Black had made a bargain with the devil 'cause his family lived high on the hog when everybody else had nothing. Old Thomas even sent his younguns off to fancy schools," added Davey.

"Maybe the Blacks were just better farmers," offered Cassie.

"Hah! That's just it. The Blacks didn't hardly farm a'tall," Davey said. "Mam says they magicked up their money. Made a bargain with the devil. And cursed us."

"Well, my family hasn't made any bargains with the devil," Cassie declared.

"Hey, we don't believe this stuff," Daisy said hastily. "You just wanted to hear about the feud."

"Besides, it's fun to listen to Mam's tales. I wish you could come over and hear her. She's a good storyteller."

"Maybe I'll turn myself into a . . . moth, and fly over some night."

"You be sure and tell us when you're gonna do it," Davey advised, "so I won't swat you."

Daisy giggled. "Now every time I see a moth I'll think of you."

Davey stopped picking the scabs on his knees and stood up. "Hey, I got an idea. Let's pretend we're Indian trackers, using our signs. I'll go first and you-all try to follow my trail."

"Sit down, dummy," Daisy ordered. "We have to make up the signs first."

"Let's make 'em up while we play. I've got ants in my pants from sitting so long."

Davey looked so miserable that they agreed.

All afternoon they tracked one another through the woods. Once Cassie led them dangerously close to the house and they had to stay flattened in a ditch while Jason ran the tractor around the field. Justin was watching, which made their escape more difficult.

"Boy, that was close!" Davey said when they were safely in the woods again. "Those your brothers?"

"Yeah. Justin and Jason. They're twins, too."

"They're a lot older'n you, huh?"

"By seven years. A lot smarter, too. They're going to college this fall on full scholarships."

"Football or basketball?"

Cassie giggled. "Neither one. They aren't into sports. They got scholarships because they're super brains. Real eggheads."

"Do they bug you like Matt and Riley do us?" asked Daisy.

"Sometimes. They sure like to tease me. But they're okay. For boys."

"Hey-y-y, watch it," Davey protested.

But Daisy laughed and nodded.

"Can you come back tomorrow?" Cassie asked when they reached the fence.

"We'll let you know," Davey said, pointing to the stones.

The next afternoon Cassie was late and angry. She was late because her father insisted on finishing the upper level of the house before lunch. And she was angry because her brothers wouldn't stop teasing her about Mr. Micawber. Even after she'd left bread crumbs and popcorn out for the crazy crow, he hadn't shown up!

She jogged along the path, hoping her friends hadn't gotten tired of waiting. Fortunately, they were just coming from the opposite direction. "Whew! I thought I was late."

"Mama was froeing. We had to help," Daisy said.

"Throwing what?"

The twins giggled. "Not throwing. Froeing," Davey said. "Making splits for oak baskets with a special tool called a froe."

"Remember we wanted to show you the basket factory?"

Cassie nodded. "Yeah, but I never saw any big buildings up here."

"It's not a big ole plant, just a shed where we work," Daisy explained. "See, tobacco's the men's cash crop. The women make baskets to sell at the Virginia Highlands Festival in Abingdon. Coles' baskets bring top dollar.''

"Me and Daisy help gather the willow whips, grapevines, and honeysuckle to make the baskets," Davey added. "Show her, Daisy."

Daisy took something from her pocket. "Lutie made this one for you. For finding Hiccup."

"It's beautiful!" Cassie examined the miniature yellow basket that fit in the palm of her hand. "Lutie made this?"

"She makes the best baskets of all," Daisy said. "But don't let on I said so. Granny thinks *she* does."

"I won't. Please thank Lutie for me."

"You wanna see how it's done?" asked Davey, his eyes sparkling.

"Sure."

"What are you up to now, Davey Cole?"

"Daddy took Cousin Matt and Cousin Riley into town. We could slip down, Indian fashion, and show Cassie the factory. Nobody'd see us."

"Cassie's afraid of the bridge," protested Daisy.

"No, I'm not. If you can cross it, so can I."

"See, smartie. Come on, follow me."

Crossing the bridge wasn't nearly so bad this time. Sneaking up on the long wooden shed was hard, but worth the effort. Cassie watched fascinated as the Cole women's nimble fingers wove baskets of many sizes and shapes.

Several times Lutie looked in their direction but didn't seem to see them. Finally, Davey signaled it was time to go and they made a dash for the safety of the woods.

"Good thing we weren't Indians on the warpath," Davey chortled. "Those women would be minus some hair."

"We'd be minus some hide if Daddy'd caught us," Daisy reminded him.

"There must have been a dozen different kinds of baskets. Why so many?"

"Folks didn't have paper or plastic a long time ago," Daisy said. "They used baskets for everything."

"There's more'n a dozen kinds, too," Davey said, counting on his fingers. "Egg baskets—one and two dozen—tater, bean, corn, apple, peach, berry, nut, flower, sewing, bread, baby, and picnic just to name a few."

"Don't forget the mule basket," Daisy said.

"You put a *mule* in a basket?"

Daisy giggled. "No, we put the baskets on the mule. Like saddlebags, one on each side so he'd carry stuff."

"Uncle Bass once had a mule who wouldn't budge an inch if one side had an ounce more'n the other," Davey said.

"Did you have to use a scale?"

"Naw. Uncle Bass'd drink some of the off-load until it weighed even."

"Aunt Stella gave the mule away and Uncle Bass didn't talk to her for a month," Daisy said, giggling. "We still have the baskets though."

Davey stopped and listened. "We'd better get back. I hear the truck."

Cassie didn't hear anything. But before she could say anything the twins had melted into the trees.

The next day when she went to the fence she saw three stones stacked up. "I hope Lutie didn't snitch on us," she muttered.

When the stones were still in place on the following day, she was really concerned. She walked all the way to the bridge, looking for her friends, but there was no sign of them.

Feeling abandoned, she ambled back to the house and sat down on the front steps.

Her mother's voice floated through the open window. "You'd really like to stay, wouldn't you?"

"Yes," her father answered. "Blackhaven feels like home. Do you realize I've never owned a piece of property, Ann? As a military brat, college student, and professor I've always lived in rented quarters."

"I know. Can't we manage?"

"If we hadn't invested most of our savings into keeping Greyfriars afloat, we could. As it is, I think we'd better put the property up for sale. That money will give us a little cushion."

"The boys will be in college this fall. How much can it cost to live here?"

"More than we can afford. You know how close we're cutting things. We need that crummy job in Vermont or we'll soon be on the dole."

"Now, Marcus . . ."

Cassie didn't stay to hear anymore. She had no idea they were in such trouble! Now she really had to find the treasure. Before, it had been more of a game. This was serious. She'd have to start all over. . . .

Chapter Nine

The Spirit Cave

"Where have you been?" Cassie demanded, seeing her friends waiting by the fence.

"Daddy took Aunt Stella to visit Uncle Bass at the prison farm," Daisy answered.

"Matt and Riley watched us like hawks for two days," added Davey.

"They would've ratted on us, for sure. We're sorry."

"That's okay. I missed you, but I've been busy, too." That was the honest truth. She'd turned Black-haven upside down and backwards looking for the treasure.

"So have we," Davey said. "We got Mam to talking again. She told us about that cave on the top of Witch Hat. Let's go see if we can find it."

"Mam said it was a spirit cave," Daisy hedged. "What if some old Indian spirits are still hanging around?"

"After all these years? Anyway, Mam didn't say they *lived* in the cave. She said the Indians sent their braves up there for special names or something."

"Hey, I've heard of that," Cassie said. "In a book I read Indian boys were sent out alone to dream dreams and get their adult names."

"See, Daisy. It's not a bad place."

"Okay. Which way?"

"To the top!" Davey replied.

Getting to the top of Witch Hat wasn't as easy as saying it. There weren't any paths through the thickets of laurel and rhododendron. Sometimes fallen trees or large boulders blocked their routes and they had to double back to find another way up the rocky crest.

On one such switchback they came upon a small spring with a crow happily bathing in the pool below it. "Shoo!" Cassie yelled. She was afraid it was Mr. Micawber. What if he landed on her arm or something? Would Davey and Daisy think she really was a witch?

"Why'd you do that?" asked Daisy.

"I wanted a drink," Cassie said, bending down and scooping water up in her hand.

"Come on, slowpokes," Davey urged. "We're almost there."

Pushing and struggling, they kept on going upward.

Finally, Davey let out a whoop. "It has to be right around this ledge on the other side."

"Why on the other side?" sputtered Daisy.

"Because, dummy, Mam said we could see three

states from the top. We can't see anything but our valley from this side. Here, I'll go first.''

"Don't, Davey!" Daisy begged, eyeing the narrow ledge. "It doesn't look safe."

Cassie wasn't too eager to venture out on the foot-wide ledge either. But Davey's *"Wow!"* made her feet move.

Daisy was close behind. "Don't look down."

"Don't worry. I'm not going to."

Suddenly the ledge widened and Cassie was standing beside Davey. Daisy joined them on the rocky apron.

"Would you look at that!" Davey said in an awed voice.

Stretched out before them were waves of green mountains, a silver, snaking river, toy-sized farms, and meandering roads. It was all breathtakingly beautiful, except for one high, barren, scarred pile of earth and rocks.

"What's that?" Cassie asked, making a face.

"Daddy calls it Purdy's Poison," Davey answered. "Sam Purdy's a strip miner. He blew up the mountain, took out what he wanted, and left this mess where nothing will grow."

The view was awesome, but it was making Cassie dizzy. "Let's look in the cave."

It wasn't much of a cave. It was merely a deep depression in the rocks, no more than ten feet wide and twenty feet deep. Crude figures were carved along the walls. The floor of the cave was littered with shards of pottery and bird droppings.

Cassie wasn't too disappointed. She'd already decided there was no way Aunt Twyla could have gotten up here to hide anything.

Daisy picked up a decorated piece of clay. "This looks just like a piece of that pot Mam has in her room!"

"Do you suppose Great-grandpa Albert stole it from here?"

"Could be," Daisy said, giggling. "Maybe he didn't want to come home empty-handed."

"I don't believe he chased a deer up here, that's for sure," Davey said.

Something about the cave was making Cassie nervous. She felt as if they'd broken into a church. "Let's go. We've seen everything."

"I'm ready," Daisy agreed.

Even Davey looked a little jittery. "I'll go first. Let's do it this way," he said, spreading his arms and facing the mountain.

"You next," Daisy said to Cassie.

The ledge looked smaller from this angle. Cassie stepped out and began inching along. A sharp crack, followed by a loud rumble of rocks, froze her. *"Davey!"*

"Go . . . back. . . . The ledge . . . fell. . . ."

Cassie stepped back into Daisy's arms. Neither of them breathed until a chalk-faced Davey came inching toward them. His whole body was trembling as they dragged him inside the cave.

"How bad is it?" Cassie asked when she found her voice.

Tremors still ran over Davey's body. He answered through clenched teeth. "Pretty bad. About three feet . . . maybe four . . . fell off on this side."

"Can we jump the gap?" Daisy asked.

Davey shook his head. "We might land on air."

"How about the top?" Cassie ventured.

"After I stop shaking, let's try it," Davey said. But once he went out and looked upward he changed his mind. "It's no good. See how it curves out? Even if you could get a good grip, you'd be hanging out in space."

"So what do we do?"

"We could yell. Maybe someone will hear us."

They yelled until their throats ached. Only the wind answered.

As the sun set behind Witch Hat and dusk settled over the valley below, they fell silent. Huddled with her thoughts, Cassie wished with all her heart that she hadn't been so secretive. It had kinda been fun to do something forbidden . . . something no one knew about. But now she was paying a high price. Unless they could jump that gap, they were stuck up here forever.

Daisy put an arm around Cassie's shoulders. "Don't be sad, Cassie. They'll find us."

"Yeah, Daddy'll track us up here. He's a better tracker than any Indian. He'll get us out," Davey said confidently.

64

"Does he know you've been coming on Black property?"

The twins looked at each other, hope draining from their faces.

"Maybe this time Lutie will tell on you," Cassie said, putting on a brave smile.

Davey perked up. "That's right! When the chips are down, Lutie will tell."

To help pass the time as dusk turned to night, Cassie swore the twins to secrecy and told them about Aunt Twyla's letter.

"Wow! That's neat," Daisy said. "Have you found anything yet?"

"Not one single, solitary thing. Mom says Aunt Twyla meant the beauties and treasures of nature."

Davey blew a raspberry. "Grown-ups have no imagination."

"I hope they have enough to imagine where we are," Cassie said.

Chapter Ten

Rescue!

A golden crescent peeked over the horizon. It grew into a yellow ball, chasing away the mist lingering over the valley.

Cassie watched the sun's progress as she tried to stretch her cramped muscles without waking the twins. They'd talked most of the night.

A shadow suddenly blocked the sun.

Cassie closed her eyes. She couldn't believe what she saw.

"Caw-aw-w," said the figment of her imagination.

"Mr. Micawber?"

The bird strutted on the edge of the ledge, looking at her with bright eyes.

"You do turn up at the oddest times. Come on in, Mr. Micawber."

He hopped closer.

She felt rather than saw the twins wake up. "Be

still," she whispered. "This is a 'sometimes' friend of mine."

Mr. Micawber cocked his head and inspected the twins.

"Come on, Mr. Micawber," Cassie crooned. "We need your help. We're stuck up here and nobody knows where we are." She held out her hand. "Come to Cassie. They won't hurt you." Daisy and Davey seemed to be frozen in place. She couldn't even hear them breathing.

Mr. Micawber flew up and perched on her arm.

"This is Mr. Micawber, guys. Remember the letter? I think he was Aunt Twyla's pet. This is Davey and Daisy, Mr. Micawber. You've seen us together, haven't you?"

"Caw-aw-er," said the crow, walking up on her shoulder.

She could feel his feet clutching gently through her T-shirt. "Think, guys," she begged.

After a long pause, Daisy whispered, "Your hair ribbon."

Cassie saw the possibility. "Right. Untie it, Daisy."

Very carefully, Daisy untied Cassie's ponytail.

"Can you tie the ribbon around his leg? I'm sure Mom will recognize it, if she sees it. Will you let us do that, Mr. Micawber?"

Mr. Micawber shifted from one foot to another, but he let Daisy tie the ribbon.

"Oh, what a good friend you are. Now don't play

games this time. Let somebody see you. Lead them up here. Okay?''

"Caw-caw-caw," Mr. Micawber cried and flew straight into the sun.

Cassie turned to find her friends staring at her with a mixture of wonder and fear. "No, I'm not a witch! Neither was Aunt Twyla. Lots of people have pet birds."

"I've heard of canaries," Daisy said, "but never crows."

"I never heard of a girl who talks to birds. I just hope he understood and gets us out of here. I'm hungry," Davey said, stretching.

Cassie's stomach rumbled in agreement.

"We'll give Micawber a little time and then we'll start yelling again," Davey said.

It seemed to be a long, long time before someone answered their shouts.

"We're coming! Hang on!" Mr. Black called.

"We aren't going anywhere," Cassie answered.

"Anybody hurt?" Mr. Cole yelled.

"Nope. We're fine . . . just hungry," Davey answered.

"I don't like the looks of that ledge. We'll try over the top. Watch for a rope, Davey."

"Yes, sir."

They watched and waited. But when the rope appeared it was too far out for Davey to grab it. A few minutes later Mr. Cole yelled, "Davey, can you hear me good?"

"Yes, sir."

"Here's what I want you-all to do. Get in a line. Cassie, you're the lightest. You go first. Then Daisy. Davey, you're the anchor. Hold on to Daisy's waist. Daisy, you hold Cassie. Now, Cassie, come out on the ledge—just till you can see me. Okay?"

"Okay," Davey called. "Here we come."

"Walk easy. . . . That's far enough. . . . Cassie, I'm gonna throw you this rope. You catch it. Daisy and Davey'll hold you steady. Hold your hands out."

Mr. Cole sounded so calm and sure of himself that Cassie wasn't too afraid. She held out her hands.

Mr. Cole tossed the rope right into them. "Loose the slip knot and put the rope over your head and under your arms. Let go of her, Daisy. Now, come on, jump. We'll catch you."

Cassie took a deep breath . . . looked at her father's white face . . . and jumped. Only her toes hit the other side. But the rope tugged her over and into her father's arms.

Once more the process was repeated and Daisy was safely across. Davey stood alone with no one to anchor him.

"Just hold one hand out. I'll put the rope right on it," Mr. Cole said confidently.

Cassie saw the beads of sweat on his brow and knew he wasn't as calm as he sounded. But his throw was perfect.

Davey put the rope under his arms. With a broad grin, he jumped, landing solidly with both feet.

The ledge broke beneath him.

Davey plummeted downward, but the rope held him. In the silence that followed, they heard rocks tumbling and crashing down the steep slope.

"Why'd you go and jump so hard, you young fool?" Roscoe Cole asked when Davey was hauled up. Sweat—or was it tears—ran down his cheeks.

Davey looked embarrassed. "It—it's a special place. I didn't want anyone to disturb it again." He looked at the six-foot gap and shivered. "Now no one will."

Roscoe Cole just shook his head. "Fire a shot, Riley. Let Dulcie and Ann know we found their strays."

Riley fired a shot into the air. "Yahoo! Get along, you little strays. We're heading home for food and bed."

"I could sure eat!" Davey said.

"I hope you can do it standing up," Mr. Cole growled. "I've half a mind to thrash your butts."

"Only mine, Daddy. It was my idea," Davey said quickly.

"We went along with your idea. We're guilty, too," Cassie said.

"That's right, Daddy. Cassie and I are just as much to blame as Davey."

"Whoo-ee! Would you listen to 'em? All of 'em want a whipping," Matt cried.

"A little taste of hickory might do wonders. . . . If nothing else, it would knock some smarts into you,"

70

Mr. Cole said. "Trouble is, hickory makes the wrong end smart."

It took Cassie a minute to get the joke and join in the laughter. Laughing made her feel better. If Mr. Cole could make jokes, then he wasn't really angry. She hoped the same held true for her family. Her father hadn't let go of her hand since he caught her. He didn't look angry, just awfully tired. There were deep blue circles under his eyes. Her brothers seemed no different than usual, as they plowed down the mountain with Matt and Riley.

Going down Witch Hat didn't take nearly as long as going up. Before she knew it, her mom was hugging her so tightly she thought her ribs would crack. The twins got the same treatment from Dulcie, in spite of Davey's squirming.

The Coles refused Mrs. Black's offer of breakfast and drove away.

Now that Cassie was safe her mother remembered she was angry. "Why did you do such a foolish thing, Cassandra Black?"

"I'm sorry, Mom. We didn't know it was foolish or dangerous. We were just curious about the Indian cave."

"Why did you deliberately deceive us about the Coles?"

"Because you'd already decided you didn't like them and you hadn't even met them."

Jason grinned sheepishly. "She's got you there, Mom."

"That's no excuse for breaking your promise, Cassie. Dulcie said you'd been over to visit them. You promised to stay on our property."

"But I had to go! I had to return Hiccup."

Mr. Black rubbed a hand over his baggy eyes. "You had to return a hiccup?"

"Sure, Dad," Jason said. "If you borrow a hiccup, you certainly should return it."

"I didn't borrow him. Hiccup's Lutie's dog. Daisy said he was the runt of the litter . . . no bigger than a hiccup. He got lost and I found him."

"All right, Cassie. Take it from the top," her father said wearily.

Cassie launched into her story. When she came to the part about their secret signs and tracking games, Jason started laughing. "So that was it! You had us running in circles half the night. Mr. Cole finally figured it out. He said it was a game you were playing."

"Go on, kitten. And, please, keep it short and to the point."

Cassie told the rest quickly. "So what do you think of the Coles now?"

Mrs. Black smiled. "Roscoe Cole scared the wits out of me when he appeared at our door and growled, 'I come for my two.' But during the night I learned to appreciate him. I liked Dulcie, too. I would have gone crazy without her calm."

72

"Do you suppose the Coles have been getting a bum rap?" her father asked.

"What does that mean?" asked Cassie.

Mr. Black stood and stretched. "Reputations are easy to get and hard to lose. Maybe all of the Coles don't deserve their reputations."

Cassie nodded, then giggled. "Remind me to tell you about our reputation."

"You mean about the Blacks being witches?" asked her mother. "Dulcie told me about it last night. It seems silly today, but I suppose it didn't years ago. People make up stories to explain what they don't understand."

"Speaking of stories," Jason said, "I'm sorry I didn't believe you about Mr. Micawber, Cass."

"Ditto," said Justin.

Mrs. Black laughed. "As long as I live I'll never forget Mr. Micawber landing on our clothesline with that red ribbon tied around his leg."

"I'll never forget the expression on Roscoe Cole's face," Mr. Black said. "But he caught on and followed that crow before we had stopped gawking."

Cassie saw her chance and took it. "Okay. If you believe Mr. Micawber, do you believe there's a treasure?"

"Give us a break, Cass," Justin said, groaning. "Can't you see how poor Aunt Twyla was?"

"She didn't even have a phone, a TV, a VCR, or a microwave," Jason pointed out.

"I'll bet Mr. William tells us something different when he gets well," Cassie said stubbornly.

A funny look came over her father's face. "Cassie, we heard from the attorneys yesterday. Poor Mr. William died. His son Bill will handle our affairs now. Bill made no mention of a treasure of any sort. I'm sorry to spoil your fun, kitten."

Suddenly Cassie felt very tired and sad. "I wish I could have met Mr. William. He was Aunt Twyla's friend. I bet he was neat."

"I'm sure he was," her mother said. "Now let's all take a nap and we'll feel much better."

Cassie stumbled upstairs to bed. All the joy had gone, just like air from a balloon. A piece of the puzzle was permanently missing. Somehow, like Aunt Twyla, she'd counted on Mr. William. Now she was all alone in her belief of a treasure.

Chapter Eleven

Treasure Hunters

"Did you get a whippin'?" Davey called as Cassie approached the fence.

"No. Did you?"

"No, we got a talkin' to. That was almost as bad."

"Granny said we didn't have the sense God gave a goose," Daisy said. "And that's pretty stupid."

"My family still thinks I'm being stupid about the treasure."

"We don't!" Daisy said. "We talked it over. A treasure makes sense. That's why the Blacks didn't want folks on their property."

"Explains where they got their money, too," Davey added. "We'll help you find it."

"You will?"

"Sure as shootin'! Every kid in the world wants to find a treasure. We're lucky. We got one to look for."

Joy and hope flooded through Cassie. Now she wasn't

alone. "Where do we start? I've looked everywhere I can think of."

"We search for her hidey-hole."

"What's a hidey-hole?"

Davey sighed impatiently. "This treasure's probably so big you'd need a big place to hide it. Right? Well, a cave would be perfect, *if* you had one. But, if you don't, you make one like moonshiners do. It's a man-made cave."

Cassie wasn't about to ask how he knew about moonshiners! "I see. Let's get crackin' then."

The twins looked sheepish. "We can't today," Daisy said. "Daddy gave us extra chores. How about tomorrow?"

"Okay. Come as early as you can."

The twins dashed off and Cassie went home. The house was quiet except for the clatter of her father's typewriter. She grabbed some cookies and went to her room to read.

She had just settled down when Mr. Micawber lit on the window sill. In his beak was a piece of green glass. He deposited it and looked at her expectantly.

"A trade, huh? Okay, fair enough. You deserve it." She raised the screen and exchanged a piece of cookie for the sliver of glass.

"Caw-aw," said Mr. Micawber. He took the cookie and flew away. A few minutes later he was back with a pretty yellow pebble.

She gave him the last of her cookies. "All gone. See?"

Mr. Micawber pecked up every crumb and flew away. Cassie put her treasures in her little yellow basket and went back to her book.

Early the next morning there was a knock on the back door. "Can Cassie come out and play?" asked Davey.

"We did our chores so good Mama gave us the whole day off," Daisy explained as they hurried off down one of the paths.

Davey pulled a paper from his pocket. "I made us a search map. We mark off each section as we look."

"Cool!"

Treasure hunting was slow, knee-skinning, scratch-getting work. By late afternoon they'd covered only a small area on the map.

"Don't be down, Cassie," Daisy said. "It won't be easy to find something hidden by a smart lady like Miss Twyla."

"I didn't expect it to be easy," Cassie grumbled, inspecting the second gash on her knee. "I just hope I have enough blood to last."

Slowly, but surely, they marked off each section of the map. Cassie thought they were past the witch business until one afternoon the twins came over with two strange bags tied around their necks. "Phew! What are those?"

"Garlic," Daisy answered. "It's supposed to ward off a witch's spell."

"See, Mam threw a hissy-fit when she heard we've been comin' over here," Davey explained. "She wouldn't stop her caterwauling till we promised to wear them."

"We didn't say for how long," Daisy said, removing her necklace and hanging it on the fence. "Let's get going. Granny says her bones are aching something fierce. That's a sure sign we're in for a storm."

"We only have the Plum Creek section left," Davey said, consulting the map. "I saved the best for last. Lots of rocky places for a cave down there."

But there were no hidey-holes by Plum Creek. Cassie plopped down under a tree and handed out some candy bars. "What do we do now?"

"Maybe you should go through the house again," Daisy said. "Or under it."

"Under . . ."

"Sh-h-h!" Davey hissed. "I heard something down by the creek."

In the quiet they heard the distinct rattle of bushes.

Daisy shrugged. "It's probably those deer we saw earlier getting a drink."

Davey stood up and peered through the trees. "No it isn't! I saw somebody dressed in camouflage."

"You reckon Matt and Riley are spying on us?"

Davey shook his head. "Too big for them. And they don't have any gear like that. Let's go see." Without waiting for an answer, he took off through the woods. Cassie and Daisy followed. But when they reached the creek no one was there. The woods were strangely silent.

"You made me snag my shirt," Daisy complained. "There's nobody but us around here."

"Not now," Davey said, pointing at the creek bank, "but there was." In the damp soil was a long, narrow boot print.

"That's not Matt or Riley," Daisy said. "They have lots wider feet. I never saw anybody with feet that narrow."

"It's not Jason or Justin either."

"It's a man's boot though," Davey said. "Running, too. He didn't want us to see him."

"Who could it be? What was he doing?" Cassie asked. The hairs on the back of her neck began acting in a familiar way.

Davey scowled. "This isn't the first time I've felt like somebody was watchin' us. I thought it was your brothers, Cassie. I bet somebody else is looking for Miss Twyla's treasure."

"Get real, Davey," Cassie said. "Nobody believes there is a treasure but us."

"I wouldn't be too sure of that," Daisy said. "Folks around here aren't dumb. They knew the Blacks got their money from somewhere."

"I thought you said people believed we were witches."

"Some did. Some didn't. But I bet everybody suspicioned there was something secret on Witch Hat Mountain."

Cassie nodded. It made sense. Her father said the few

people who had come to look at Blackhaven were more curious than interested in buying. "I did feel someone watching me when we first came. Remember, I thought it was you? Then I thought it was just Mr. Micawber flying around."

"Whoever it was is up to no good," Davey said. "Honest folks don't go sneaking around on private land."

"I'm going to tell my parents," Cassie said as thunder growled in the distance.

"We'd better run. Granny's bones were right," Davey said.

Cassie was only too glad to get out of there. The three of them took off at a rapid clip.

As soon as they were out of sight a camouflaged figure rose from behind a boulder not ten yards from where the three had been sitting. The figure stared after the kids for a long time, then turned and trotted off in the opposite direction.

"Tomorrow," Cassie called, taking the path toward Blackhaven.

The family was sitting on the porch when Cassie ran up. "Man in . . . camouflage . . . sneaking . . . by creek . . . weird . . . footprint . . . ran like . . . a deer."

"Catch your breath, Cassie," Mr. Black said, laughing. "It was probably just some hunter who strayed."

"*No!* Someone's trying to find Aunt Twyla's treasure!"

The twins threw their hands up in horror. Justin jumped to his feet, shouting, "Circle the wagons! Blackhaven is under attack!"

Jason dropped to one knee and peered through the porch rail. "Man the guns! Someone's making off with our land. Shoot the varmint!"

Even her father and mother were laughing!

Cassie exploded. "Stop it! I hate all of you eggheads! You think everything I say is a joke. And that's when you decide to listen to me. Well, I'm not a clown! This isn't funny!" Without waiting for a reply, she ran inside and up to her room, slamming the door behind her. She was so mad her whole body was shaking.

A few minutes later Mrs. Black came into the room. "Cassandra, that was a terrible display of temper. What's wrong?"

"I don't belong in this family."

"Tell me what you mean by that, Cassie. Please?"

Cassie sat up. With a catch in her voice, she said, "I'm not a teacher, a writer, a painter, or a—a genius. I'm just a clown everybody laughs at. I don't fit in this family."

"Oh, Cassie. I've never heard anything so ridiculous. So you aren't any of the things you mentioned. Everyone—including the twins—is different. You are a very important member of this family. How could you think you don't belong?" She reached out to Cassie, but Cassie drew away.

"Forget it."

"Cassie, you're obsessed with this idea of a treasure. I know you have a wonderful imagination, but this isn't rational."

"I didn't imagine Aunt Twyla's letter."

"No, you've chosen to misinterpret it. Now I think it's time you stopped this nonsense. You've become quite different lately."

"Lately? I'm always the different one."

"What are you talking about, Cassie?"

"I just told you," Cassie said, flinging herself on the bed.

"I want *you* to forget this treasure business," Mrs. Black said. "In fact, I don't want to hear that word again. Do you understand?" When Cassie didn't answer, she said, "When you can apologize for your behavior you can come downstairs." She went out, closing the door behind her.

The day had become as dark as Cassie's mood. She curled up on the window seat and watched the storm. She'd never felt quite so alone and angry. What was happening to her? Usually she just shrugged off her brothers' teasing. Why, all of a sudden, did it matter so much? Never before had she screamed at her parents. The very thought of her behavior made her stomach queasy. Lost in her thoughts, she didn't hear the door open again.

"Hey, Cass."

"Can we come in?"

"Why not?" Cassie said, feeling angry all over again.

"Don't you want some light?"

"No."

"We're sorry about teasing you, Cassie," Jason said.

"We didn't mean to hurt your feelings."

"Well, you did."

"Yeah, we know."

Cassie glowered at the twins. "Why doesn't anyone ever take me seriously?"

Her brothers exchanged looks. "Cassie, you operate on a different wavelength, for sure," Jason said. "And you shoot ideas at us like machine-gun fire."

"If I didn't talk fast I'd never get a word in edgewise, not with you eggheads."

"Eggheads respond to logic," Justin said. "Try starting at the beginning of your story instead of the middle. Your mouth starts running before your brain's in gear."

"You might also consider that our viewpoint could be right," Jason said.

"Yeah? Like how?"

"Okay. Let's say there was someone in the woods. Even a strange footprint. What makes you so sure it was someone looking for Aunt Twyla's treasure? Why isn't it more logical that it's a stray hunter, like Dad said?"

"And, for another thing, why do you persist in believing there *is* a treasure?"

"Because Aunt Twyla said so!"

"Hey, we all read the letter. You're the only one who thinks that way. With all your searching, have you found anything?"

"No, but—"

"Come on, Cassie. Can't you see why we keep teasing you?"

"Give over, Sis. The treasure is all in your awesome imagination."

"Mom and Dad are really worried about you. They have enough problems without this. Come downstairs and make nice, Cassie."

How do you convince somebody about something you feel in your bones? Especially without proof. Could they even be right? It was four against one. Cassie sighed. "Okay. Guess I just got carried away."

Flanked by her brothers, she went downstairs and apologized.

Her father looked relieved. "It's okay, kitten. We shouldn't have laughed at you. We also shouldn't have let it go this far. We were too busy with our own things to correct you. I agree with your mother; no more talk of treasure. No more searching. Just enjoy the time we have left. Agreed?"

Reluctantly, Cassie nodded. "Yes, sir."

Chapter Twelve

The Curse

"I think the sky has a hole in it," Cassie grumbled. "It's been raining for three whole days."

"Radio said clearing later," her father assured her.

"I sure hope so. I'm down to my last book."

The sun came bursting through the clouds just as she finished the last page. "I'm going over to the Coles'," she yelled. Grabbing her windbreaker she hurried through the rain-slick woods. She wasn't sure how the twins would take the new restrictions. Of course, they hadn't spent all their time looking for the treasure. But it had added a touch of excitement.

Crossing the swinging bridge over the roaring river was excitement enough to last her all day. Her heart was pumping about a hundred miles an hour by the time she reached the other side. It barely had time to slow to normal by the time she reached the Coles'.

Mam sat alone on the wide front porch. As soon as

her watery eyes recognized Cassie, the apron went over her head.

"Good morning," Cassie said in her most polite voice. "Where is everybody, Mam?"

Mam began rocking. "Don't hurt my kin," she said in a quavery voice.

"I don't want to hurt anyone. I want Daisy and Davey."

"Take back yer ole jar. Albert never shoulda tuk it," whined Mam. "It were the onliest gift he ever give me."

So that was it! Albert *had* taken a pot from the cave. "I don't want the Indian jar, Mam. I want the twins."

The rocking stopped. "Don't take 'em! Take the jar. And take off the curse. Us Coles have suffered enough." Under her apron Mam was shaking like a leaf in a high wind.

Cassie felt sorry for her. The poor old woman really believed the Coles were under a curse, and that she was a witch. What could Cassie do to make her feel better? After a moment, an idea popped into her head. Standing tall, she intoned in her most dramatic voice, "I, Cassandra Black, remove the curse on the Cole family. I declare all is right between us. So be it."

"Mam, who you talking to?" called Lutie, as she limped toward the porch. "You need anything?"

The apron came down. Mam gave Cassie a timid, toothless smile. "I'm fine now, child. Cassandra Black's

86

come t' call.'' She began a slow rocking rhythm and her head fell slightly forward.

"Hi, Cassie," Lutie said. She adjusted the shawl around Mam's shoulders. "Poor old thing. I'm glad you made peace with her. She's been real worried about the twins. You come to see them?"

"Yes. Are they around?"

"Just follow your nose to the kitchen. I'm gonna grab a fresh breath."

Cassie followed a tangy aroma to the big, black-beamed kitchen. Clouds of steam rose from the pots boiling on the wood stove. The Cole women bustled about, snapping beans and filling the rows of glass jars.

"Hi, Cassie," called a pink-faced Daisy. "Have a seat—if you can stand the heat."

Cassie sat beside Daisy and grabbed a handful of beans to snap. "Where's Davey?"

"He's lucky. He's helping Daddy load the truck. He should be back directly. What's up?"

"I need to talk to you."

Daisy put aside her beans and brushed back a damp strand of hair. "Come on, we'll go out back."

"Is it okay?"

"Sure. I'm due a break. How'd you get by Mam without her throwin' a fit?"

Cassie followed Daisy to the back stoop. "Oh, she did. But I used my awesome imagination. What's been put on can be taken off."

"Huh?"

Cassie told her about removing the curse.

Daisy laughed so hard tears ran down her pink cheeks. "Boy, I can't wait to tell Davey. Wish I'd been there."

"That's the good news. The bad news is that we can't hunt for the treasure anymore."

"Why not?"

Cassie explained the result of her temper tantrum.

"What did they say about the man we saw?"

"Dad says it was a stray hunter."

"Hah! What was he hunting? No game's in season."

"It doesn't matter," Cassie said. "I'm not allowed to think, speak, or look for the treasure. Can you come over tomorrow anyway?"

"We were coming over later this afternoon," Daisy said looking a little upset. "We wanted to say good-bye. We're going to Abingdon in the morning to get ready for the festival."

"How long will you be gone?"

"A little over two weeks. We're staying with Grandma McDonald."

"We may be gone by the time you get back!"

"Yeah, that's what Davey and I figured. Do you think your family would come to the festival? There's lots to do: Barter Theater, art and antique shows, games, food, and stuff."

"Maybe. I sure can try."

"Hi, Cassie. You get tired of waiting for us?" Davey

said, plopping down on the steps. "Boy, I never saw so many baskets. The truck's plumb full."

"You didn't pack the you-know-what, did you?" Daisy asked in alarm.

" 'Course not," Davey said with a grin. "I'll go get it. Be back in two shakes of a lamb's tail."

It may have been a trifle longer, but he returned very quickly with something held behind his back. "Here," he said, thrusting a basket at her. "Me and Daisy made this for you."

"It's made from the honeysuckle vines you helped us gather, remember?"

Tears stung Cassie's eyes. "Yeah, I remember. Thanks. It's really beautiful. I'll keep it forever. I—I don't have anything to give you."

"Hey, you gave us the best summer we ever had," Davey said.

"That's right. We didn't find Miss Twyla's treasure, but we sure had fun trying, didn't we?"

A lump that felt as big as a cantaloupe rose in Cassie's throat. All she could do was nod. She stood up, hugging her basket. "I better go. You're busy."

"Tell Davey about Mam first," Daisy said. "We'll walk to the bridge."

Finding her voice, Cassie told Davey what she'd done.

"Wish you'd thought of it sooner," Davey said, laughing. "I hated that stinkin' necklace."

"Try to get your folks to come to the Highlands Festival, hear?"

"Dad's working nonstop on his book and Mom's trying to finish the painting of Blackhaven before we leave. No one seems to have time for fun things. But I'll try. Have fun in Abingdon."

"Don't forget us," Daisy cried as Cassie jauntily crossed the bridge.

Cassie turned and waved to the twins before diving quickly into the woods. She didn't want them to see her cry. She wondered if she'd ever see them again.

Chapter Thirteen

Witch Hat's Secret

She made the discovery by accident.

Feeling at loose ends without her friends, Cassie wandered into Aunt Twyla's room one afternoon. Nothing in the room had changed all summer except today the room seemed to welcome her. Cassie stood before the left bookcase and read the titles out loud, *"Flowering Plants; Birds of the Blue Ridge; Songbirds; The Geology of Appalachia; Gold Mining; The Carolina Goldrush; Mountain Wildflowers; Botany; Medicinal Plants."*

Well, it figured. Aunt Twyla was a naturalist. But there wasn't anything here she wanted to read. Sighing, she moved to the other side of the fireplace. More of the same!

The room felt stuffy and hot. Cassie raised two windows and sat down at the desk. Absently, she pulled out Aunt Twyla's worn address book and thumbed through the pages. The *B* section was the fattest. Aunt Twyla really had kept up with Grandpa Charles! Each old address was carefully marked out as a new one was added. There were addresses for Dad, too, ending with Greyfriars. The only other entry under *B* was an old one, judging by the faded ink: John Jacob Browne Company, Assayer, 1234 Seventh Street, Washington, D.C.

Cassie reached for the desk dictionary. ASSAYER: One who analyzes ore for quality and content. The idea that flashed in her mind was so outrageous she laughed out loud. Was there gold at Blackhaven? That would explain all of Aunt Twyla's books on gold. Hey, Cassie thought, my awesome imagination is really working overtime! Gold on Witch Hat Mountain? Where did that idea come from? No way. Gold was found out west . . . California . . . New Mexico . . . Alaska. . . .

Almost as if someone had propelled her, she rose and walked to the bookcase. Her eyes focused on *The Carolina Gold Rush*. Her heart beat a wild tattoo as she pulled out the book. It fell open to an underlined passage:

Coldspring, North Carolina, Jackson County— 1855: In this small community on the north side of the Blue Ridge, two men found gold in a stream of a spring. The spring gushed up through a rock and each morning at the foot of the spring they could pan a penny weight or so of gold. Not satisfied with this amount, one of the men decided to blow the rock apart and get all of the gold, and this he did. Somehow, though, the course of the spring was changed and no more gold ever came forth again.

Shaking, she forced herself to scan the whole book. Yes, gold—a lot of gold—had been found in the Blue Ridge Mountains. Before the Civil War there had even been a United States Mint in Charlotte, North Carolina. Was it possible? Was there a spring on Witch Hat that gushed gold? Had Aunt Twyla been afraid someone would blow up her mountain to get more? She dropped the book and flew to her room.

The little basket sat on her dresser. Nestled inside were some of the yellow pebbles Mr. Micawber had bartered for cookies. Were they gold nuggets? How could she tell? Gingerly, she picked them out from the other treasures. They felt warm on her palm. Maybe another book would tell her how to determine if they were really gold. She dashed back across the hall. The book she had dropped and pages lay scattered on the floor!

"Oh, gosh! I broke Aunt Twyla's book."

She stooped to pick up the pages. Except the loose sheets weren't from the book! It was a letter. The back endpaper had been lightly glued with the letter inside. The fall had shaken the inserted pages loose. She recognized the flowing script. And it was addressed to her! Her knees gave way, and she sank in a heap on the floor and began to read.

Dear Cassandra,

Against William's advice I'm leaving this letter and book for you to discover. With it you can solve the mystery of Blackhaven. We Blacks are not witches as people were led to believe. However, Witch Hat Mountain has always been a unique place. Even the Cherokees recognized that.

It was my father, Thomas Black, who found the little spring. He, too, was a naturalist and was more concerned with protecting the many natural treasures of the mountain than he was with becoming wealthy. With the help of an old friend, John Jacob Browne, he was able to use the gold and keep his source a secret.

The spring has yielded smaller and smaller quantities of gold as the years have passed. It has been enough for my needs, plus a small surplus which I have invested. However, if the secret were known some greedy individual might be tempted to blow the mountain apart to find the source.

When I visited with your family I felt all of you might benefit from Blackhaven's riches. You are the rightful heirs. However, should you choose to sell the property, the remainder of my estate will revert to the National Wildlife Foundation.

My one request of you is, if Blackhaven is to be sold, you destroy this letter and book. Without these I believe Witch Hat's secret will remain hidden. I make this request because of late someone

*has been prying into my affairs, and I am uneasy
about my mountain's fate. Be guided by Mr. William's sound advice.*

Yours affectionately,
Aunt Twyla

The letter fell from her hands. "Things didn't work
out like you planned, Aunt Twyla." What to do now?
Cassie chewed her lip for a moment, then got up and
straightened the bookshelf. Taking the book and the
letter, she went to her room, stuffed everything in her
backpack, and set off to find the spring.

It took some time to locate Mr. Micawber's bath
again. But after several false tries, she found it. The
clear, cold water bubbled from between two large gray
stones into a shallow basin. It flowed a few feet and
disappeared under another pile of rocks. It did not reap-
pear on the other side.

"Awesome," Cassie murmured, dipping a finger into
the water. Some golden flecks swirled away from the
disturbance. "I guess a chunk washes out every now
and then. But how did Aunt Twyla ever manage to get
way up here?"

"Caw-caw-er," scolded Mr. Micawber from his
perch on one of the boulders.

"You did try to help me, didn't you? You are a good
friend, Mr. Micawber. I'll bet you know how she got
the gold, too, don't you?"

The crow stared at her silently.

"Where does the water go?" she asked, walking around the pile of stones below the spring. Clambering to the top of the heap, she looked down the mountain for any sign of a stream. Nothing. Just a bird's eye view of the backyard and the shingled roof of the troll house . . .

A grin spread over her face. "The Blacks did work magic, didn't they, Mr. Micawber? They made water disappear!"

Mr. Micawber bobbed his whole body in agreement.

Cassie jumped from the pile of stones and raced down the mountain, her backpack thudding between her shoulders. Boy, was her family ever going to be surprised!

Grabbing a broom from the back porch to fend off any lurking spiders, she went down the stone steps of the springhouse. The door creaked open. Cool air flowed out to meet her. She knelt beside the trough where the water entered and rammed her hand back into the opening. Her fingers felt a screen! *Bingo!* This had to be the way the Blacks collected the gold. Using both hands, she pulled gently. The fine mesh filter came out easily. Tiny golden chips and a few larger pebbles remained as the water seeped away.

"Pretty neat, Aunt Twyla." She took out the larger stones and slipped the screen back in place. "Witch Hat's secret will be safe with us. I promise."

"Playing house with the trolls?" Jason called as she emerged into the bright sunlight.

"You almost missed all the excitement," Justin said. "Dad found a buyer. He and Mr. Purdy are going over the sales papers right now."

Cassie felt a chill run down her spine. "Who is this guy Purdy? Where'd he come from?"

"He's a mining engineer who used to live in Trinity. Wants to move back to be near family," Jason said to Cassie's retreating back. "Hey, what's your hurry?"

The name Purdy had put Cassie on alert. She ran full tilt into the living room. Her parents were sitting on the sofa reading some papers. A very large, smiling man filled her father's easy chair.

Everyone looked up as she skidded to a halt.

"What is it, Cassie?" asked her father, frowning.

She couldn't speak. Her eyes were riveted on the fat man's feet. His long, extremely narrow feet!

"Cassie?"

"Family council," she croaked. "I call a family council."

Chapter Fourteen

The Last Surprise

"Can't it wait, kitten? Mr. Purdy and I have some business to finish."

"Won't take a second," Mr. Purdy said, looking at Cassie with bright, beady eyes.

Cassie had felt the force of those eyes before. "No. The rule's the same for everyone, isn't it, Dad?"

"She's right," Justin said from the doorway.

Reluctantly, her father rose. "Excuse us for a few minutes, Mr. Purdy. We have this family rule . . ."

"Go right ahead, folks. Humor the little lady." His lips smiled, but the smile didn't reach his eyes.

"Where to, Cassandra?"

Silently, she led them to the room off the kitchen. Her mouth was dry. Fear made a hard knot in her stomach. How could she make them listen? Justin's words echoed in her head: "Eggheads respond to logic. Put your brain in gear before your mouth." She would have to try. Aunt Twyla was counting on her. "Shut the door, please, Jason."

"This had better be important, Cassie," her mother warned.

"It is." Unslinging her backpack, she took out the letter and *The Carolina Gold Rush*. "Would you read the underlined passage out loud, Dad?"

His mouth set in a grim line, Mr. Black read the passage about the man finding a spring of gold. "All right. What's the significance?"

Cassie pulled the nuggets from her pocket. "This is the Black treasure. There's a spring here just like in the book."

"Are those for real?"

"Naw! Only fool's gold."

"Sh-h-h!" begged Cassie. "Not so loud."

"Everyone be quiet," ordered Mr. Black. "Cassandra, whatever gave you this wild notion? Just because you read something in a book doesn't mean it applies here."

"Yes, it does. This letter was hidden in the book. Read it, Dad, and you'll see."

He read the letter quickly. "This is unbelievable! How did you come across—"

"How doesn't matter right now. What's important is that you don't sell Blackhaven to Mr. Purdy. He's the guy who's been snooping around here."

"How do you know that?"

"Because of his feet! They're super long and narrow. Just like the footprint we saw at the creek."

"His feet are pretty odd, Dad," Jason said. "Didn't you notice?"

Mr. Black rubbed a hand over his eyes. "Springs, gold nuggets, and odd feet. I don't believe any of this."

"It's true. Honest! I can prove it. The Blacks piped the spring down to the troll—uh—springhouse. You can see for yourself," Cassie said, beginning to panic.

"And somehow Sam Purdy caught on? Is that what you're saying?" Jason said.

"He doesn't have to know exactly what the treasure is. Just that there is one. I know he's the watcher in the woods."

"Maybe that's why he wanted to buy the place 'as is,' Dad," Justin said.

"I suppose that's possible. He made a point of saying he hadn't been up here since he was a young boy delivering firewood to Miss Twyla. His footprint tells a different story. There's something rotten in the state of Denmark."

"I don't know about Denmark," Cassie said. "But something sure smells in the state of Virginia."

"The matter certainly deserves investigating. Let's put Purdy on hold," Mr. Black said, opening the door.

As they filed out, Justin winked at Cassie. "That's the way to handle eggheads, Cass. Everything calm, cool, and collected."

"Thanks. But I don't feel calm or cool. I'm about to shake into a million pieces."

100

Jason took her arm. "Lean on me, kid. Dad will take care of this dude."

Mr. Purdy welcomed them back with a jolly smile. "That didn't take long. Ready to sign, Mr. Black?"

"I'm afraid not. Cassandra pointed out to us that Aunt Twyla specifically asked us to wait until we talked with her lawyers before we made any decisions."

"I talked with Bill Frawley yesterday," Mr. Purdy protested. "He said you had decided to sell."

"Nevertheless, we are going to honor my aunt's request. Surely a day or so won't matter?"

Mr. Purdy snatched the papers from the table. "It's now or never, Mr. Black," he said angrily.

"Then it will have to be never. Good-bye, Mr. Purdy."

Mr. Purdy looked stunned. "Now, wait a minute. Let's not be hasty. You could lose a lot of money here."

Mr. Black said nothing.

"You found out, didn't you?" Sam Purdy growled.

"Found out what?"

"Don't play games, Mr. Black. The Indian name for this place is *Wampugansit*—gold mountain. It doesn't refer to the mountain at sunset or any other such rot. There's gold under here. Right?"

Her father actually had a look of surprise on his face. "Good gracious, Mr. Purdy. That sounds like a wild tale my daughter would think up."

101

Sam Purdy looked as if he might explode. "It isn't a wild tale, I assure you. I'm a mining engineer. As partners, we could both make a bundle from this mountain. You're making a big mistake not dealing with me."

"I've made a few mistakes in my time," Mr. Black said, "but this isn't one of them. Good day, Mr. Purdy."

Red-faced, Sam Purdy stormed out.

Cassie's legs gave way, and she collapsed on the sofa.

"Way to go, Dad!" Justin said. "Hey, let's see those stones again, Cassie."

"How much do you think they're worth?"

"What do we do now, Marcus? We certainly can't sell to that awful man."

"First," said Mr. Black, "I want to know how you made this discovery, Cassie. Whatever gave you the idea of gold in a place like this?"

"Aunt Twyla and Mr. Micawber nudged me in the right direction when the time was right," Cassie answered, expecting everyone to laugh.

No one did.

"We still have a problem Aunt Twyla didn't foresee," her father said.

"Perhaps not," Mrs. Black said. "What about the estate Aunt Twyla mentioned? How much is it? Would it be enough for us to live on for a while? And why weren't we told about this?"

"There's only one way to get answers to those questions," Mr. Black said. "I'm going to find a phone and talk to Bill Frawley."

Each minute seemed an hour long while they waited for her father to return. Jason and Justin tried to keep her occupied with questions, but she was too jittery to enjoy her unaccustomed spot in the limelight. At the first sound of a car all four of them rushed out on the front porch.

"You're not going to believe this," Mr. Black warned, bounding up the steps. "Aunt Twyla's estate is well over a quarter of a million dollars!"

"Get real!"

"Oh, yes. Bill Frawley said Miss Twyla was a very frugal lady and a wise investor. And he was *very* surprised that we didn't know the terms of her will. He assumed his father had explained everything to us by correspondence. When we put Blackhaven on the market Bill Frawley thought we'd chosen to leave and give the estate to the National Wildlife Foundation."

"Did he mention the gold?"

"No. I think Aunt Twyla and Mr. William played things very close to their chests."

"You mean we'd have lost all that money and Blackhaven, too, if it hadn't been for Cassie?" Justin said.

"I'm afraid so," Mr. Black said, smiling sheepishly. "If it hadn't been for her persistence we never would have discovered *all* the treasures of Witch Hat Mountain."

"Does that mean we get to stay?" Cassie asked, finally breathing normally.

"Yes. There will be Blacks at Blackhaven for some time to come," her father said.

Cassie bolted down the steps.

"Where are you going?" her mother called.

"To find Mr. Micawber and tell him the good news!"

This time no one laughed at the girl who talked to birds.